Identity Crisis

Jayne Osborne

Published in 2025 by FeedARead.com Publishing

A CIP catalogue record for this title is available from the British Library.

Dedicated to Christine, with love and thanks for her help, suggestions and friendship.

Chapter One

The dark bulk of the football stadium loomed over Alexandra Taylor as she made her way past it on her journey to her flat. On match evenings, it was illuminated, and she felt safer when walking past it, but tonight, as there was no match scheduled, it was dark and she hurried to go past. Her day had been long, and she wanted to get home. Not that there was anything to get home for, she thought to herself, as she turned the corner – supper, TV and then bed as usual. The streets were dark, as it was the end of October, the street lights didn't give a lot of illumination, and the darkness had fallen long before she left her office, and to complete her misery, it had started to rain. She increased her speed, as the rain got heavier, and reached the front door of the house where she lived. She opened the door to enter, removed her coat, and shook the rain off it, before shutting the door behind her. As she put her foot on the first step, the door behind her opened, and her landlady came into the hallway, and smiled at her. She was carrying a bottle of milk, and she held it out to her. "Hello Alison, good day?"
"Yes thanks Mrs. M. Busy as usual. Everything alright today?" she asked, for the landlady had not been well lately. "Yes, thanks dear. I've got your milk here. That milkman's getting later every day, so I thought I'd better bring it in for you."
"Thanks Mrs. M. I'll see you later" she said, as she made her way upstairs. She closed the door of the flat behind her, and hung the coat on the hanger on the back of the door, before going across to the

small fridge, and placing the milk in it. The routine of making herself a drink, before she got on with cooking her meal followed, and she sat down wearily in the easy chair, to drink it. By the time she'd cooked her meal, eaten it and cleared away, she went to have a shower, and got ready for bed, before she watched a programme on the television. She took a good look at her hair colour in the mirror when she got out of the shower. It didn't need to be dyed again before Christmas, she thought to herself. She was a natural blonde, but for several months now, she had dyed it light brown, and it did change her appearance. It still gave her a shock, when she looked in the mirror, but at least it served its purpose, and to her colleagues at work, who had never known her anything but a brown-haired woman, they did not think of her as anything else. She was of medium height, had blue eyes, with shoulder length hair which she wore in a French pleat, and she was slim, almost thin, for she had lost a lot of weight in the past few months. Now, she sat down and turned the television on, but the programme she had wanted to watch had been replaced, and she didn't like the replacement, so flicked the remote control to try and find something else, and sat up with a shock as she came to a programme on the country's economic state, and saw a familiar figure on the panel. She couldn't help herself, she turned the sound up, and watched entranced as the man spoke. He was in his mid-thirties, had short dark hair, dark brown eyes, was remarkably handsome, was very well and expensively dressed in a well-cut suit, white silk shirt and a dark silk tie, and as he moved his hand, she could see he was still wearing his wedding ring. She looked down at her bare hands, she had removed hers, when she left him, but she admitted to herself, she still loved him. She sighed, and knew she wanted to talk to him again, but was reluctant to do so, for he had hurt her badly, and she couldn't face him, without getting too emotional. The programme came to an end, and she turned the set off, and went to her bed. She lay in the darkness, trying desperately to dispel the memories that had come after seeing the programme, but at 3.00 a.m., she gave up, turned the lights on again, and went to make herself a cup of tea. She took it back to her bed, and sat up against the pillows, thinking about him.

She had first met Damien Ellis, when he had been admitted to the surgical ward where she had been working as a staff nurse, when she had been on duty. He had gone to the theatre that afternoon, for the removal of a very nasty inflamed appendix, and she had been on hand to care for him, when he returned to the ward. They had become friends in the short time he had been in hospital, she had looked forward to going on duty just to see him again, and before leaving the ward, he had asked for her phone number. She had given it to him, but hadn't expected to meet up with him again, and when he phoned a few days later, she had jumped at the invitation he had issued to go out to dinner with him. They had married within six weeks of their meeting – a whirlwind romance, and she had known that she loved him with all her heart. She had been on her own, for she had been bought up in a children's home, after her parents died when she was younger, and didn't have any other relations of her own. Damien was an economist, working with a company that advised the government, he was often busy in the public eye, and couldn't spend vast amounts of time with her, but she hadn't been too worried. She had been introduced to his housekeeper, and had seen the way the woman looked at her, but nothing detrimental had been said, and indeed, she had been glad to get to her new home after her duty, to Damien and a cooked meal, and hadn't had much to do with the woman. She had insisted on working out her notice at the hospital, and Damien had been unable to get time off, so they hadn't had a honeymoon until they had been married for nearly two months. Finally able to take time off together, they had flown to Scotland, for she hadn't wanted to go abroad, indeed, she didn't have a passport, and he had hired a car and they had toured around the islands of the Inner and Outer Hebrides and she had loved every minute of the weeks they had spent together. They had visited Mull and Skye, before going onto The Outer Hebrides, driving northwards visiting Barra, the Uists, the Isles of Lewis and Harris, and then taken a good deal of time on their way back to London, exploring Northumberland and the Lake District as they drove back. When they got back from their holiday, and started their married life together, she had discovered to her horror, that there wasn't anything for her to do in the flat where they were living, for the housekeeper, did everything, not allowing her to do anything, certainly no housework or cooking, and accustomed to being busy all day, she felt bored. The flat was luxurious, but she often felt trapped in it. She had told him how she felt, but he had laughed, telling her not to bother her pretty head about it, just enjoy spending some time with her friends, and telling her she would have enough to do when the children came along. She had laughed at his comments, for she did want children, but not for a while, until they had spent more time together. He had showered her with gifts and clothes, given her a fantastic allowance, and would take her out whenever he could, but somehow, those occasions hadn't happened very frequently, for his work became more intense and he was often late home, and some nights he would stay at a hotel to be on hand when he was needed urgently. But, in addition to those times, he often had to go abroad on various trips for the Company, and she wasn't able to accompany him. Indeed, he didn't seem to want her to go with him, telling her she would be on her own, for he wouldn't be able to spend a lot of time with her, and although she had protested that happened all too frequently anyway, he didn't change his mind, so she stayed at the flat, alone again. Her friends at the hospital had been so envious of her, and her new lifestyle when they first heard about it, but they didn't contact her after their return to town, and her friendships with the girls she had trained with, had seemed to die after she married, she had little or no contact with them, despite phoning them frequently, and she had got progressively lonelier without anybody to talk to.

She sighed as she remembered the arguments they had started having as time passed - she had accused him of not wanting to spend time with her, while he had retaliated saying she didn't want to be seen with him, when he had to attend receptions, and indeed, she didn't like going to them. She had looked forward to accompanying him, when they went to the first one, but soon realised that they weren't her cup of tea. Every one she went to, was full of elderly, pompous men, who had their wives with them, also elderly and pompous, but also unfriendly, and she didn't get on with any of them. She seemed always to be the youngest person present, and she wasn't able to make conversation with the older women, for they had formed their own little cliques, and she was excluded from them. If they did talk to her, they seemed to talk about nothing but their grandchildren, the difficulty of finding reliable help in the house, or the luxurious holidays they had been on, and didn't allow her to contribute to the conversation at all. Then there were other receptions which she hated even more, full of foreign business men, who were accompanied by their wives, none of whom spoke any English at all, and her schoolgirl French was not enough so they could talk together, so she was left on her own again, while Damien and the other men would talk together, disappearing into a different room, only reappearing after a long interval, so all she wanted to do was get home and away from them, as quickly as possible. They had been married for nearly eight months, and she had begun to wonder if she had made a mistake in marrying him, for they hadn't been out for an evening together for a while, and she began to feel that her new life was a complete waste of time, so she had been delighted when she was told of an orphanage nearby, where she could do some voluntary work. She had returned to the flat, pleased with the prospect of being able to do something useful again, but that evening, when she had informed him that she was going to start working with children, he had put his foot down, insisting that she didn't need to do anything like that, saying she wouldn't be available if he wanted to take her on holiday at a moment's notice if she were working. She had protested at that, trying to persuade him, that as she was a volunteer, she wasn't going to be tied down to regular hours, but he was insistent, and although she had resented the amount of control he seemed to want of her life, she had reluctantly informed the orphanage she would not be able to join them. They had argued even more after that, but she had resisted the urge to disobey him, and waited to be taken away. Needless to say, they hadn't gone anywhere, and she had resented him even more. When she had asked him when he would take her away again his answer was that he was very busy, and she would have to wait. Their sex life was marvellous, when they were able to be together, but one evening, when he had returned from a foreign trip, and they were spending a rare evening alone together, she had asked him to spend more time with her, he had told her that he was incredibly busy, trying to help the government of the day, and wasn't able to do so. She had accused him of caring more about the government than he did of her, and not wanting to be with her, and they had argued violently, although they had made up their disagreement in bed later on. It was the day after that argument, when he told her at breakfast, that he would have to meet up with some government members, and thought that the meeting would probably run very late, so he would stay in a hotel, so as not to disturb her, and would not be home until late the following day. He had kissed her goodbye before leaving, and she had looked after him, wishing he would, just for once, not go into the office, but stay with her. Unwilling to sit alone in the flat again, for the housekeeper was never keen on her spending time in the apartment, she had decided to go shopping instead. The flat they lived in, was in Richmond, so she hailed a taxi to take her into Knightsbridge and the West End. Her shopping spree was enjoyable, she had enjoyed buying some clothes in Harrods, her parcels were to be sent to the flat, and she had felt able to relax a little, so after a quick lunch in the restaurant, she decided to walk some of the way, looking in shop windows to see if she fancied anything else before she got a taxi back to the flat, and set off. She had been idling along, looking in the windows of John Lewis in Oxford Street, and had gone to look in one of the windows in the side road, and was thinking about going home, when a taxi drew up near her, and a smartly dressed woman got out. She was extremely pretty, slender and wearing a designer suit, with a smart hat perched on her dark curly hair, and looked the very epitome of elegance. Alexandra had noticed her elegance, and now she watched without much interest, as the woman asked the taxi driver to wait, while she walked a little way up the road to one of the small green spaces that were dotted all over London. Her interest was piqued by a suit in the window of the shop, and she stepped into the doorway, to examine it properly, and looked up again, in time to see Damien run to the woman, clasp her to him, and kiss her with a great deal of passion, before they got into the taxi and were driven away. Alexandra was white with shock, for she hadn't expected anything like that to happen, and resolved to talk to Damien about it when he came home again. Her shopping was forgotten, she hailed a taxi, and was driven back to the flat. When she got there, she phoned his office, but his secretary informed that he was unavailable, in meetings for most of the day, would be in meetings at the hotel that evening, and probably wouldn't be free to phone her until the following day at the earliest. She had asked the woman to get him to phone her as soon as possible, replaced the receiver with a sigh, and went into the sitting room to sit and think about what she had seen.

She had forgotten that Damien wouldn't be home that night, so was in a bad mood all evening, thinking about what she had seen, trying to read, and failing miserably, then trying to concentrate on her embroidery, but unable to do so, and spent a sleepless night. When the sun came up in the morning, she was tired, her eyes heavy, wanting to talk to Damien, but at the same time not wanting to hear that he was tired of her, and steeled herself to talk to him when he did appear. He didn't phone in the morning, and when contacted, his secretary informed her that he was in meetings, and she knew she couldn't stay in the flat all day, for the housekeeper appeared in the doorway, enquiring when she was going to go out, so eventually, put on her coat again and went out, walking slowly through Richmond Park, wondering what Damien would say when she asked him about the other woman. She walked until she was tired, before turning for home. She had reached the exit, when a taxi drew up outside the hotel opposite the park entrance, and the same woman got out, followed by Damien. She drew back into the shelter of a tree, and watched as he paid off the taxi, took the woman's hand, and they went up the stairs to the hotel, their arms around each other. She stood for a while, just watching, but they didn't reappear, and finally she turned, walked back to the entrance she had entered the park from, and went back to the flat where she avoided the housekeeper and went to their bedroom.

She sat on the bed, staring at nothing, just wondering what she was going to do. It was obvious that Damien was having an affair with the woman, and wondered how long it had been going on. In the end, determined she was going to talk to Damien, she picked up the phone, and dialled the number of the hotel. When it was connected, she asked if Mr. Ellis were a guest at the hotel and was informed that Mr. & Mrs. Ellis were definitely guests, and was asked if she wanted to be connected to their room. She agreed, but when the phone was answered, and she could hear Damien saying 'hang on darling,' before he said 'hello?' she found she couldn't speak, and put the phone down without speaking. She was crying, bitter tears at the destruction of her dreams for the future, and knew what she had to do. She wasn't going to stay here, a prisoner in the flat, with nothing to do, but wait for her cuckolding husband to appear and let her be the second best in the marriage. Her shopping from Harrods had been delivered that morning, but she didn't even unpack it, just left the boxes on the floor, and instead, packed a couple of cases with clothes – ordinary, everyday clothes, for she knew she would have to get a job to support herself, and left all her evening dresses, bar one, on the rails. The evening dress she put in the case, was light green, very simple, gathered under the bust and hanging to the floor, together with matching shoes and was the first outfit that Damien had bought her, and she didn't want to leave it behind, for it had a very special memory for her. She didn't want to be beholden to Damien for anything, and put her cases in her wardrobe while she went out. She wasn't going to leave him, until she had found somewhere to live, and without seeing the housekeeper, left the flat again. She eschewed her local shops, knowing that if Damien were to try and find out where she had gone, he might enquire at the places, but travelled further up the Thames to Teddington, and found a local paper shop, which had details of flats for rent in the windows. She scrutinised them, and found one that would suit her. She was lucky, for the flat she found, suited her very well, and she paid a deposit on it. Her new landlady was Mrs. Megson, and she knew that she was very lucky to have found somebody who would let her share her house. The flat wasn't ideal, a bedroom, sitting room, small bathroom and a small kitchen attached to the sitting room, but it was going to be hers, and hers alone. She resolved to find a job, so she could support herself, and never have any contact with Damien again. And she had done just that. She had left a note for Damien, the writing of which had caused her a lot of pain, but eventually she had been satisfied with it. She recollected now what she had written -

"Damien, I'm sorry, but I can't stay with you anymore. I thought you loved me, but it's obvious you don't anymore, if you ever did. I had thought that we would be happy together forever, but when I saw you with that woman, you looked at her as you used to look at me, so I don't think we could ever be happy again. I wish you had been able to tell me that I wasn't your first love, for I could probably have forgiven you, if it had only been once, but when I saw you together again, well, that was it! I don't know how long the affair has been going on, but I don't think you ever loved me enough, and you've now realised you made a big mistake in marrying me, and you've been using your job as an excuse for not spending very much time with me. I'm not taking anything from you, as I'll be able to get a job quite easily. I've left all the jewellery you gave me in your dressing table drawer. Perhaps your new girlfriend would like it? Don't try and get in touch with me again. All the best for the future. Alexandra

She had pinned the note onto his pillow, picked up her cases, let herself out of the flat without seeing the housekeeper again, left her keys behind, and walked away from her life as a married woman.

She had decided not to go back to work as a nurse again, but instead found a job as a secretary to a consultant surgeon who worked in the local hospital. She had trained as a shorthand typist when she was in school, before she started her training, and now it came in useful. She had tried to change her appearance as much as possible, just in case she met up with Damien again, but as they had very rarely visited Teddington when they were together, she didn't think it would be likely that he would come to the area, and she had decided to change her name, and was now calling herself Alison Turner, instead of Alexandra Taylor. She was earning a good living as a secretary in the hospital, was able to pay her rent, and although she had told him not to get in touch with her, she had realised he had continued to pay her allowance into her bank account. She didn't touch it, just left it where it was, knowing she would eventually return it to him, but she admitted to herself, she was lonely for Damien, and missed being with him. Now, she laid down again, turned the light off again, and finally she slept.

The following morning, she had woken heavy eyed, after her almost sleepless night, and walked to the hospital where she worked. One of her fellow workers, Delia, looked at her as she sat down at her desk, and her eyes widened. “Ali, what on earth's the matter? You look as though you haven't slept for a week. Are you alright?” Alexandra nodded and yawned. “Didn't sleep too well last night” she admitted. “Had something on my mind, and ended up having to make a cup of tea at three o clock this morning, in an effort to try and get off to sleep.” Delia looked at her and grinned. “Will you be able to stay awake today?” she asked, “After all, you're working for Mr. Williams, and he's enough to make anybody fall asleep, the way he works.”

“Oh, don't remind me” she groaned. “I ought to have thought about him last night, when I was trying to sleep. That should have sent me off without any problem at all.” The surgeon in question was elderly and slow, and took absolutely ages to dictate his notes. “When does he go” she asked now, for the man in question was due to retire soon, and Patricia, the supervisor in the office joined in the conversation “Didn't you hear? Today's his last day. He's retiring sooner than expected, and they have appointed somebody who starts very soon.”

“So, who am I going to be working for after today?” she queried, and Patricia smiled “You're going to be in the pool with the other girls, until the new man starts, and you'll probably be working for him.”

“Well, thanks for telling me” She was indignant. “After all, I've been working for Mr. Williams since I arrived, and I didn't know any of this. Why wasn't I told?”

“Don't know why management didn't tell you, but it won't make much difference will it?” Patricia shrugged, and Alexandra decided it wasn't worth the hassle to argue with her. Now, she went to put the kettle on for coffee, before the day's work began, and made drinks for the rest of the girls in the office. She wasn't busy during the day, taking a small amount of dictation from Mr. Williams, who thanked her for all her hard work, and telling her that he was going to recommend that she take over his work with the new man. She was sad to see him go, when he signed the post for the final time that day, and wished him a very happy retirement as she said her goodbyes to him for the last time.

By the time she reached her flat that evening, she was tired after her sleepless night, and after exchanging some small talk with her landlady, and cooking herself a small meal, she showered and went to bed. The following day, she wasn't working, for it was the weekend, so she did her food shopping for the week ahead in the local shops, went back to the flat to put it away, before going out again for a walk. The day was overcast again, but she felt that she needed to get away and get some fresh air. She had walked in the local park near her flat, and decided that whatever the weather, tomorrow she would go for a long walk by the river.

It was as she was making her way home, that a woman walking in front of her, slipped, fell over, and injured herself, twisting her ankle quite badly. Alexandra ran to help her, for although she wasn't nursing now, she still retained her skills, and it was obvious that the woman needed help. "I'm Alison

Turner" she introduced herself, "And I'm Emma Davies" was the reply. By the time the ambulance had arrived, it was dark, but they had made friends, for despite her injuries, Alexandra knew that the woman wanted to talk "I hope this isn't too bad" Emma said, as they waited for the ambulance. "I've only just got a permanent job. I've found a job as a housekeeper, with a really nice man, who's had a lot to put up with recently, so I'd like to stay with him if possible."

"I don't think it's too serious" Alexandra tried to reassure her. "You'll be back on your feet quite soon, and hopefully, your employer will be good enough to let you recover at your own pace." The ambulance arrived and as Emma had told her she didn't have anybody of her own, she accompanied her to the hospital. She waited to find out how Emma was, promised to come and visit her on the following day, said her goodbyes and made her way home.

The next day, she went to the hospital to visit Emma, and after spending a while, trying to find the ward she was in, for she worked in a different part of the hospital, and very rarely left the offices, she finally found it, and spent a while with her, just talking about things in general. "Will your employer be okay with you staying in hospital for a couple of days, as you've just started working for him?" she asked, and Emma nodded. "He's working abroad for a few days, so he's away at the moment" she answered. "His wife left him, then his housekeeper walked out on him, because he tried to blame her for some of the problems his wife had been having, so he's become very busy with his work. Trying to forget things, I expect. He's talked to me occasionally, and I think he's quite lonely, since his wife left him. Poor man, he's really good to me. I've been told I'll be able to go home tomorrow, so I'll be there when he gets back from his foreign trip."

"Would you like me to contact him tonight and let him know where you are?"

"No, it'll be okay thanks. As I say, he's away, abroad for a while, so it will be alright thanks. But you must come and visit me and meet him."

"Sure," Alexandra agreed. "Give me your address, and I'll come and see you sometime." Emma nodded, and Alexandra produced her notebook. "Write it down in here, and I'll make some arrangements" she suggested, and watched as Emma wrote the address in her book. She was about to take a look at the address that had been written, when the Sister approached, and she was asked to leave, for the doctor wanted to examine Emma, so putting the notebook in her handbag, she said her goodbyes, and promised to see her again. It was as she was walking down the corridor from the ward, that she heard voices behind her, and turned a corner, to find that she had gone the wrong way, and retraced her steps trying to find the entrance, just in time to see Damien and another man walking away from her. She knew she had lost colour, and stayed where she was, leaning against a wall, as she regained her breath. He had looked the same as he had done when they were together, just more tired than usual, and his hair had a small amount of grey in it, and she was grateful that he hadn't seen her. Finally, she regained her composure, found her way out of the hospital, and walked swiftly home to the flat.

She had forgotten about going for a walk now, and sat instead, drinking the tea she had made. Finally, she reached into her handbag and found her notebook, opened it, and looked at the address that Emma had written. She glanced at it, and groaned, for there written clearly, was the address of the flat she had lived in with Damien. Oh no, she thought, with despair, Emma was Damien's new housekeeper!

She spent another disturbed night, wondering how she was going to avoid meeting up with Emma again, just in case Damien was to appear, and came to the conclusion that she would have to lose contact with the older woman. She was sorry about that, for she had got on well with the older woman, and had wanted to maintain her ties with her. She did wonder why Damien had been in the hospital, for he had looked healthy but came to the conclusion that he had been visiting, had returned from his trip, heard about Emma's accident, and come to see her. She would have to be very careful not to make her way into the main body of the hospital, just in case she saw him again. Finally, she was able to sleep, and woke un-refreshed, to go to work the following morning. During the day, she typed a letter to Emma, and addressed it to her at the flat, posting it on her way home. In it, she wrote that she'd had to leave the area for a while, and wouldn't be able to catch up with her again, hoped that her health was satisfactory, and said she would hopefully contact her when she got back. She was thankful she hadn't given Emma her own address, but was sorry that she wouldn't be able to meet up with the older lady again.

The week was very long and boring, for she was only doing routine work, but she wasn't sleeping properly, and she was tired when she got home on Friday evening. She knew that she would have to keep working, and decided that nothing was going to stop her going for a long walk, so after filling her Saturday with the normal tasks, she managed to sleep. She was able to think things through properly and clear her head after another long walk on the Sunday, and managed to tire herself out, so that she slept well that night. She had wanted to contact Emma, and felt bad that she had not done so, but was afraid to telephone just in case Damien was there. On the Monday, she had gone to work, to be told that her new boss would be starting that day, and she would meet him soon. She was prepared for a meeting with the new man, and had returned from her coffee break, to be told that she needed to go to Mr. Williams office, to meet him. She gathered up her notebook and pencils, went down the corridor, knocked, and on being bidden to enter, opened the door, to come face to face with Damien!

Chapter Two

Alexandra went white, as she stared at her husband, but he was smiling at her, holding out his hand to shake hers. "Hello, Miss Turner," he said slowly, "I'm Jerome Ellis, your new boss." Weakly, she shook his hand, but couldn't take her eyes off his face. He was identical to her husband, but his hair was slightly lighter than Damien's, and he had a some grey in it. He was frowning now, as she stared at him, and she shook her head, to dispel the image of her husband from her eyes. "Sorry," she said now, "you just remind me of somebody. I thought you were him, when I first saw you but he's not a doctor."

"You must be mistaking me for my brother. He's Damien Ellis, the economist. Do you know him?"

"No," she fibbed and shook her head. "I've seen him on television, that's all. You're very alike, you know." He smiled at her explanation, "We're identical twins, that's why." She breathed a sigh of relief, as she pulled herself together. "Oh, that explains it. Sorry, please call me Alison."

"I've got quite a bit of work to do, despite the fact that I've only just started here. Are you able to do shorthand and audio typing. I did specify I needed somebody who could do both, but I know what the National Health Service is like for ignoring consultant's special requests." She smiled as she answered. "Like everywhere else, I expect. But, yes," she said, "I'm qualified for both of them, so whichever you prefer, I can do."

"Great" he said, "I've got a couple of tapes here

already, and I was hoping you could take some dictation for me?"
"Of course," she answered "That's what I'm paid for." He gestured for her to take a seat in front of him, and she opened her notebook, and prepared to take dictation. Her heart rate had settled, by the time he had finished dictating his letters to her, and she was able to return to her desk in the typing pool knowing that she was going to enjoy working hard again. She was not so certain about working with Jerome however – it was like looking at Damien again, and she didn't know whether she would be able to cope with it. She was surprised when Patricia told her that she would be moving into a different office, as Mr. Ellis had wanted her to be undisturbed by the others in the typing pool, so before she started transcribing her shorthand, she moved her belongings into the small room which she had been allocated, and got started on her work. Jerome had given her a couple of audio tapes as well, so when she had finished typing the letters, he had dictated, she hooked up the audio machine, and started listening to it. Luckily, her new bosses voice was different to Damien's, the timbre was different, and she thanked heaven, for she didn't think she could have continued working with him, if his voice had been the same as his brother's. It was going to be bad enough working with him as their faces were so alike, she thought, and hoped she'd be able to cope. She listened for a moment, as he gave his instructions via the audio tape, and wondered for a moment, why Damien had never said that he'd got a twin brother. He'd told her he had a large family,

three brothers and two sisters, but never mentioned that one of his brothers was his twin! She wondered if they got on well together, or if they'd had a disagreement, which meant that they didn't see each other too often. She knew that their mother lived in the Algarve, which was why he hadn't seen her very often, but he had mentioned on one occasion that he had visited when he was in the area, that his father was dead, but she hadn't been told anything else about his family. She had never met any of them as they hadn't been able to arrange a date to get together, and the one time that some of the other members of the family had been in the country and he had arranged for a meeting, Damien had found it necessary to rush off to Brussels for a top-level conference, so the meeting had been cancelled, and after that, they had never managed to meet up with anybody else. She sighed as she put some more paper into the computer printer, to print his letters off. She had managed to try and put Damien to the back of her mind for over seven months, and now in the past three weeks, she'd met up with his new housekeeper and now she was going to work with his brother! Life, she thought to herself, is getting complicated!

That evening, she walked back to her flat, thinking about her day, for it had been busy, and full of surprises. The audio tapes had contained details he was writing for a book, and he needed them to be transcribed and saved for use in the future. Jerome had signed his post, and left it on her desk to be sent off, bidding her goodnight as he went, and she had been able to return his farewell with a smile. She hoped she would be able to work well with him, for on the first day's showing, he seemed to be a good boss. As she cooked her evening meal, she realised that it must have been him she had seen when she had left Emma, and heaved a sigh of relief that it hadn't been Damien. She wondered about his home life, and knew that she would hopefully be able to find out more about him. By the end of the week, she knew that she enjoyed working with Jerome. He was an exacting boss, knowing what he wanted and insisting that it be done that way, but he hadn't made any outrageous demands on her, and she had enjoyed his first week. And the following weeks were just as good. From comments made in the canteen, he had made a good impression on the other clerical staff, the nursing staff liked him, and he seemed to be popular with the other medical staff.

It was getting near Christmas now, and Jerome had announced his intention of having a party for the staff he worked with so he could meet them away from the hospital, and had issued a general invitation to every member of the typing pool, and other staff he worked with. The party was to be a masked ball, with identities being revealed at midnight, and lots of the girls in the pool were making plans for exotic masks. Alexandra had found a full-face mask, which managed to hide her face completely. She wondered if she would need to be hidden, but she didn't think that Damien would appear at the party, for he would probably be abroad again. She was also eager to meet Jerome's wife. She had been told that the woman was a model, named Pandora, and meant to be a recognised beauty, appearing frequently in Harpers and Vogue. She was glad she had bought one evening dress with her – she didn't want to think about buying another, for she didn’t go out very frequently, and was glad that she would have a dress to wear. She had the matching shoes with it, and when she tried it on, she realised that although it had looked good on her when she had blonde hair, it went just as well with her new hair colour. On the day of the party, she had eaten a small meal at lunchtime in the canteen, not wanting to cook anything for herself before she went out, and she was able to get home in plenty of time, and get ready to go out. She showered, washed her hair, and after drying it, she pulled it back, away from her face, and allowed it to rest on her shoulders, a different style to her normal way of wearing it, changed into her green dress, then opened her small jewellery box. She took out her favourite earrings – Damien had bought them for her when they were on their honeymoon, in the Outer Hebrides. They were of local stone, not valuable, but extremely pretty and unusual, and he had given them to her, along with a matching necklace. She loved them, and was glad she had remembered to bring them with her, for she had left everything else behind, including her ruby and diamond engagement ring, and the matching necklace and earrings, which had been his wedding present to her. She looked at her wedding ring which she was keeping in the box, and felt a pang of regret as she fingered it, but took a deep breath, shut the box again, and put it away. Now, she hooked the earrings into her ears, fastened the necklace in place, then shrugged into her coat, picked up her handbag and her mask, and went out into the street to where her taxi was waiting.

As the taxi drew up outside Jerome's house, she put her mask into place, and got out. Her friends from the typing pool were easily recognisable by their loud voices, and she joined their laughing happy group, as they went into the main room of the house, after depositing her coat with the others in the entrance hall. Jerome was standing by the door, greeting everybody who entered, trying to guess the identity of everybody who came in, but when he tried to see who she was, she laughed and pulled away from him, leaving him wondering who was behind the mask. Some of the staff were easily recognisable to her, but mostly she did not have any idea of who was hiding. There didn't appear to be any sign of Jerome's beautiful wife, but there was a woman standing by him, wearing a small mask, and although her dress was lovely, it didn't really suit her, and she didn't think she was model material, and she didn’t think that this was her sister-in-law, and wondered who it could be. The evening wore on, and the music was loud, and Alexandra was enjoying herself, for she hadn't been out since she left Damien, and she was dancing with a group of the junior doctors, when she happened to glance up, and saw the familiar figure of her husband enter the room. He was not wearing a mask, and his face looked grim, but he was talking to Jerome and the woman who was with him. She could feel herself losing colour, stopped dancing immediately, walking away from her partner, and as far away from Damien as she could get. She looked around her, but nobody seemed to have noticed him, and his similarity to their host, and she shrunk into a corner out of his line of sight. She looked at her watch, seeing the hands of it click round to midnight, and knew that she had to leave, before the witching hour, when she would have to take off her mask. Jerome, Damien and the woman, had come further into the room, so she worked her way around the edge of the room, and was able to retrieve her coat, and leave the house, without being seen by anybody. The night was cold, and she was shivering, as she reached the main road, where she was able to hail a taxi, and be driven back to her flat, where she sat, sobbing quietly to herself. It had been a mistake to go to Jerome's house, she knew that now, but she hadn't thought that Damien would attend. But he had appeared, and she knew that she had wanted to talk to him again, to find out what he'd been doing with that woman. She cried herself to a standstill as she prepared for bed, hung the dress away, and put her jewellery back into its box, before she got into her lonely bed, turned the light out and tried to sleep.

Damien turned to speak to his brother again, as they surveyed the people dancing in the large main room of Jerome's house. "So, how is Pandora?" he asked having been told that she was unwell. "She's going to be okay." Jerome replied, "She's just got a bit of a cold, and doesn't want to appear with a red nose, or a hoarse voice. Her public image is very precious to her." Damien smiled, for Jerome's voice was dry. When he had married Pandora the rest of the family had wondered how she would like living with a surgeon, but the marriage was a good and happy one, and they seemed to be as much in love with each other as they had been on their wedding day. He sighed, as he remembered how happy he and Alexandra had been on their wedding day, and surveyed the room. His gaze fell on the figure of a small woman, wearing a green dress, who was making her way out of the room, into the adjoining room, where the supper had been laid out. The dress was similar to one he had bought for his Xandra when they were first married, and had been missing from her wardrobe when she had gone, but although the mask hid her features, he could see the woman's hair, and it was the wrong colour, and a different length. He sighed, and Jerome put his hand on his arm. "You'll find her" he said for he knew what his brother was thinking. "She's got to still be in London, I reckon. She was bought up here, and all her friends are here. I don't think she'd have left the capital."

"I thought that woman who's just gone into the supper room was her, because the dress is the same colour and style as one, I bought for Xandra when we were first married, but the hair colour is wrong, and it's too long. I still have no idea who she thought I was meeting, but I know I neglected her. I wish I could apologise to her, and find out what else I'm meant to have done. She must have decided to go very quickly, because there were boxes on the floor with clothes in, which she hadn't even opened, let alone unpacked." he sighed again, "I miss her, you know. I love her so much. We had such fun when we were first married." Jerome followed his gaze. "We'll be unmasking soon, then you can see who's been hiding behind the mask. I know who you mean, but I've got no idea who it was – I tried to guess when she came in, but I couldn't." he glanced the old Grandfather clock, that stood in the hallway. "It's almost midnight, so I suppose I'd better get everybody in here, so all can be revealed." The music came to a close, and he turned the machine off, "Everybody in here, so we can unmask" he cried, and the room suddenly became crowded, as the people who had been in the supper room, came into the main room. Jerome conducted the countdown to midnight, and with a flourish, everybody removed their masks. Damien was looking around the room, trying to see the woman in the green dress, but she wasn't there, and he glanced at Jerome, who was also trying to see who it had been. "Did anybody leave?" he asked Maria, their sister, who was standing by them, but she shook her head. "I didn't see anybody go" she said, "but, there again I wasn't really watching too hard. Who were you looking for anyway?"

"There was a woman wearing a green dress, and a full-face mask. I couldn't identify her when she came in, and I wanted to see who she was, but we can't see any sign of her now"

"Oh, yes, I saw her when she came in. Nice dress, and she was wearing some really pretty unusual jewellery. She was dancing with that group of doctors over there" and she pointed out the group who had been dancing with Alexandra. Damien walked over to them, "Sorry to interrupt" he said, then grinned as Jerome joined them, and the young doctors did a classic double take. "Yes, I know, it's like having double vision, isn't it? Just wondered, if you had any idea of who you were dancing with? She was wearing a green dress."

"No," was the answer, and one young man continued "We wondered who she was, but she disappeared quite sharpish, just before midnight." he smiled, "I thought she was quite nice, and I'd have liked to find out who she was, but she's gone. She never said anything to us, didn't even tell us her name. She was a good dancer as well."

"Did she say she was going to go?" Damien asked but they shook their heads. "No, she looked up, obviously saw something which disturbed her, and suddenly stopped dancing, didn't say anything, and went into the supper room, and I haven't seen her since. I reckon she didn't work in the hospital at all, and wanted to get away before the unmasking, so she wouldn't have been revealed as a gate crasher."

"No," said Maria, as she joined the group, "she arrived alone but went over to talk to some of the other girls who'd arrived just before she did."

"Who else did you invite?" Damien asked his brother, who shook his head. "Just issued a general invitation to everybody, but not everybody's turned up. For example, my secretary isn't here tonight, but I know I invited her. Sorry Bro, I've got no idea who she was." Damien sighed, and turned away. "Hell," he said. "Oh, well, come and have a drink instead." and he stalked into the supper room. Jerome exchanged glances with his sister, and they watched as he went to the bar, and helped himself to a large Scotch. "I wish to God, he was able to find her, and find out what went wrong." Jerome muttered, and Maria nodded her head. "Who was he with? He hasn't told me much about what went wrong, and I don't like to ask him outright" she asked, but Jerome shook his head. "He says he was in meetings with government officials, and didn't go out of the office all day." he said, "but her note said that she'd seen him with a woman on more than one occasion, so I've got no idea if he was meeting anybody or not." he shook his head "He admits he neglected her, but maintains he was never unfaithful to her." He moved as if to go to his brother, but Marie put her hand on his arm "Leave him alone for a while" she said now, watching her brother, as he sipped his drink. "Get him to sleep here tonight, because I don't think going back to the flat on his own, would do him any good, and I doubt he'll stick to one drink. Pandora doesn't mind him being here, does she?" Jerome shook his head, "No, they've always got on well together, and she's gone to bed anyway, as she's not feeling too good. She's got a cold, and you know what she's like when she's got something wrong. Luckily, she's not booked for any more photographic work until after Christmas, so hopefully she'll have got over it by the time she's due to work again." Marie smiled at her brother's words, "Poor Pandora" she said. "Tell Damien he can sleep here tonight, and to remember to apologise to his new housekeeper tomorrow. Poor Emma. She'll probably have gone to bed anyway, as she's only just got over her accident herself."

"What did she do?" Jerome asked, and Maria told him the story of Emma's accident. "She said she met a really nice girl who stayed with her, took her into the hospital, and then visited her the next day, but she hasn't seen her since. She was quite upset, because she got a letter, telling her that the girl had to go away for a while, and didn't know when she'd be back, before she could visit her again. She wanted the girl to meet Damien, as she knew that he would have been pleased to say thank you to her, for looking after her."

"You've been quite friendly with her, to have learnt that lot about her" Jerome stated, but he knew that his sister was a very kind person, and had a very good heart. "Well, I went to see Damien, but he was at the office as per usual, and I got talking to Emma and found out a lot about her. I must say, she's an improvement on the one he had before. I didn't like the woman anyway, she obviously didn't like Alexandra, didn't want her around the flat, and you know Damien is putting some of the blame for Alexandra leaving onto her, because she wouldn't let her do anything around the flat. There were other reasons as well, but he wouldn't tell me about them. No wonder the poor girl was fed up. Apparently, he accused his housekeeper of acting like a jailer, and then sacked her. Not a lot is going right for Damien at the moment, is it?" Jerome grinned at his sister. "I'll get him to stay over tonight, and we can have a chat when everybody else has gone. Maybe, he'll open up a bit more than he has done recently, and then we can put our heads together and see what we can think of regarding how to find her." The party was winding down now, and Jerome was having to say his farewells to his guests, but he was able to keep an eye on his brother, and watched intently, as he spoke to one of the theatre nurses who had attended. After the woman made her goodbyes, and the room had emptied, Jerome looked around him at the chaos that remained. "I'd say leave it until tomorrow, but I can't do that to Mrs. Draper" Jerome made reference to his housekeeper. "Just give us a hand, and we can soon clear it up." and the three siblings did just that. The room was tidier when they had finished, and Maria declared her intention of going to her home to go to bed. The two men wished her good night, saw her into a taxi, locked up and went into the room that had been used for the supper, helping themselves to another drink, and going to sit in front of the empty fireplace, with its large floral arrangement. The room was warm, as the central heating had been on all night, and the chairs had been replaced in their normal positions. "So, what were you having a chat with my theatre sister about then?" Jerome asked his brother. "Is that who she was? She just said she was a nurse and worked with you, but didn't say what she did. I had asked her if she had to register to work as a nurse, and she told me she did, and gave me details of who I would have to contact. I wondered if I might be able to find Xandra that way. She's a nurse, she might be working in another hospital, for I know she's not at St. Anselm's now, which is where we met, so I was hoping to find out if there was any way I can trace her."

"And what was the answer. I must admit I don't know. The nurses have their own rules and unions, and they are completely different to the doctors' rules."
"Well, they do have to be registered. Apparently, there's a central registry, where all nurses are on a list, and it has to be checked if they start work as a nurse in a new hospital, or go to work for an agency. I wondered if I could find out, but I don't know if I'll be able to do it in the next few days, as I'll have to go abroad again very soon."
"My new secretary should be able to find out for me. She's worked in the hospital for a while, so she should have some idea. Leave it with me, and I'll have a chat with her on Monday, and ask her. I was hoping she'd be here tonight, but I didn't see her. Alison's a nice girl, but the first time I ever met her, I thought she was going to faint. She looked at me, and went absolutely white. She explained that I'd reminded her of somebody else, and when I told her you were my twin brother, she said that must have been it. Said she'd never met you, just seen you on the television. I'm not surprised she didn't turn at the party actually, apparently, she doesn't mix much, doesn't talk to anybody about herself at all, just gets on with her work and goes home afterwards, according to the other girls in the typing pool. Nobody seems to know anything about her private life at all."
"Can you ask her for me on Monday morning? As I said, I've got to go away again, so I won't be able to ask her myself, otherwise I could have come in and talked to her, and she could have had the complete

set."
"I'm not really surprised that Alexandra was fed up, you were never in the country, were you? She couldn't have had much time with you when you were home, always working." Damien nodded, looking shamefaced, as he explained. "We were really busy about that time, and I had plenty of work on, you know. I did try to spend as much time as possible with her, but it wasn't always possible."
"And how much time did you spend with her?" Jerome asked. Damien stared at the floor, knowing that his brother was right, "Not as much as I should have done" he admitted. Jerome continued. "And what about Steven? He's the one who would complete the set." he asked, for their other brother was the third member of the triplets. "Who knows where Steven is? We've been looking for ages, but never a trace of him." Damien said now, for the fact that their brother had cut himself off from the family was a great sadness to them all. He had dropped out of university, and nobody had heard from him since he left. "I think this family is fated you know. I've lost Xandra, because she thinks I was having an affair with somebody, but I have absolutely no idea who; Steven hasn't contacted anybody since he left Uni so suddenly, Mum's living it up in the Algarve, and doesn't want to come back to England, and Maria's husband is working abroad for months at a time. At least David and Elizabeth haven't got any problems that I know of. The only real success story in the family is you and Pandora." He sighed, finished his drink, and stood up. "I'm going to bed." he announced. "Thanks for the drink and the offer to

stay over. I'll see you in the morning Bro." and he went out of the room. Jerome sat looking after his brother, and thanked heaven that his marriage to Pandora was strong. He thought too, of their younger brother and sister, David and Elizabeth, who were living with their mother in the Algarve. They both loved their lives out there, had decided against coming back to the UK to go to university, but had jobs they loved, and he didn't think they'd want to return to England any time soon. He swallowed his drink, and turning the lights out, followed his brother from the room.

The following morning, as the two brothers met for breakfast, Damien looked his brother, "I couldn't sleep last night, and I got to thinking about things again, and believe me, I've done more than my share of thinking in the past. In her note, when she left me, Xandra said she'd seen me with a woman on more than one occasion. I know it wasn't me, as I was in the office all day, and I've never, ever, been unfaithful to her, I didn't meet any other women when I wasn't working, you weren't even in the country during that period, so, what do you think the chances are that Xandra saw Steven with some woman? We have no idea where he is, so he could have been in London, couldn't he?" Jerome stared at his brother, thought for a moment, then nodded. "Mother always said she could never tell you and Steven apart and she gave birth to us. I know that I'm slightly different facially to you, but you and Steven were absolutely identical in every way, although he might have changed in the intervening

years." Damien shook his head. "I don't think he'd have changed all that much. Maybe the colour of his hair, but he couldn't change the shape of his face." Jerome thought for a moment, then nodded. "It's possible I suppose. Of course, it would be great if we could find out where Alexandra saw him, but that would mean we'd have to find her first, to even try and locate Steven. I don't know about you, but I miss him. Miss the laughs we used to have, and the escapades he got up to. Mother changed so much after he'd gone, and I don't think Dad wanted to recover after his heart attack, because he'd gone. I was really worried about them both, and nothing I could do, seemed to cheer him up."
Damien nodded. "I know how you feel about it. I feel the same way too. I'd love to talk to Steven, and find out what we did." he sighed, "but as you said, we'd have to locate Xandra first. And I've been trying to do that since she left, with no luck whatsoever. I've phoned her more times than I care to admit, but she blocked my number, and now she's changed her number, and I can't contact her. I've told the private agent to forget it, and got rid of him. He was no good anyway." The door opened then, and Pandora entered the room, and Damien stood and smiled at his sister-in law. "What are you two boys talking about?" she asked, as she bent to kiss her husband. "We were wondering if Alexandra saw Steven and mistook him for Damien, and got the wrong impression." Jerome explained to his wife, and she looked slightly shocked, but nodded in agreement. "Well, I certainly can't tell Damien and Steven apart, in the photos I've seen. How long has it

been since you saw Steven?" she asked, and Jerome and Damien exchanged glances. "Fifteen years." Jerome said. "It was the end of the spring term of our third year at Uni. We'd all been to a party the night before, and we were going to go home together, the following day." Jerome said now, and she smiled as she poured herself a cup of coffee. "I'll bet you can even tell me the date" she grinned, then laughed as he nodded. "I can actually. It's not every day that your brother walks out of Uni and never reappears. But he could be around I suppose."
"If we ever find Alexandra, we'll have to ask her to explain exactly where she saw him" Pandora said, then sneezed again, blowing her nose vigorously. "How's your cold now?" Damien asked, and the talk turned to her health. "Don't give it to me thanks." Jerome said, "Or me" said Damien, as the talk became general.

After their meal, Damien said his farewells, and asking his brother not to forget to talk to his secretary, he went back to his flat. Emma greeted him with pleasure, as the door opened. "Did you enjoy the party? I guessed you wouldn't be back, but I'd left coffee on the stove if you came back and wanted it" she asked, but Damien shook his head. "Not really" he answered her. "I thought I glimpsed a woman who could have been my wife, but it wasn't her. The dress was the same, but the hair colour was wrong."
"Well," said Emma, "There's plenty of hair dyes on the market you know." She took his coat and went back to the kitchen, leaving him to stare after her, his

mind suddenly alert as he registered what she had said.

Chapter Three

Alexandra walked into the hospital grounds on the Monday morning, prior to going into work, wondering what was going to be said by her boss, as to her sudden disappearance on the Friday night. The day following the party, she had gone shopping and to the laundrette, before giving the flat a thorough clean, and making sure that she had enough food to last the week ahead although she didn't eat a great deal. The following day, after church, she went for a long walk along the banks of the River Thames, and went back to her flat, tired out, but happier than she had been for a while. On Monday though, she knew she had to go to work, so pinning a happy expression on her face, she entered the office block. Her office door was open, and Jerome was in her office, looking through some papers she had left on the desk. "What are you looking for?" she asked, and he spun round as though he had been shot. "Sorry Alison," he apologised, "I just wanted the paperwork for Mrs. Delaney, and thought you might have left it on the desk."

"No," she laughed at his expression, "I didn't want to leave the notes on show, thought it best to hide them away over the weekend, so they're in my desk drawer." and she entered her office, to open the drawer and produce the file he was looking for. He took the bundle from her, then looked searchingly at her. "What happened to you on Friday night?" he asked. "I'd hoped you'd be at the party, because I wanted to introduce you to somebody."

"Who" she asked, and was grateful she had left when she did, when he replied "My brother Damien. He wasn't going to attend the party, but he had a bit of free time, so he came to see us. You said I reminded you of him, but you'd never met him, so thought I'd introduce you, so you could see us together."

"Oh, sorry" she replied, "I found I wasn't able to attend after all. Was it a good party?"

"Yes, you missed a good time. Never mind, maybe next year." and she nodded "Maybe," she said noncommittally. She took off her coat, and hung it on the back of the door, before pushing her handbag into the bottom drawer of the desk, and Jerome prepared to leave to go back to his office, before he turned. "Could you do me a big favour, but it's not really hospital business?" he asked as he shut the door of her office. She was intrigued and looked interrogatively at him. "What do you want me to do?" she asked. He grinned at her. "I'd like you to try and track somebody down for me please. Can you contact the central Nursing authorities to find out where a woman works. Apparently, they have to verify the qualifications of any nurse who starts work in a new place, so I wondered if you can contact them, and ask where this person is working. She used to work at St. Anselm's, but she left there about 18 months ago" and he handed her a piece of paper with the name written on it, and she almost gasped when she saw her own name leaping out at her. "What's she done?" queried Alexandra, wondering why he wanted to know about her, but he shook his head. "Nothing" he replied, "Somebody wants to contact her that's all, but he can't find her."

"Now I'm intrigued" she smiled at him, "Who wants to contact her?"

"That's for me to know, and you to wonder about." Jerome smiled, "It's nothing to worry about, but if you can see if you can find out where she's working, and let

me have the details as soon as possible, I'd be grateful."
"Okay," she nodded. "I'll see what I can find out for you."
"But keep it under your hat please." he begged, "I don't want the fact that I'm looking for another woman to become public knowledge. Somebody might get the wrong impression."
"I won't say anything" she promised, and he smiled at her, as he left the office. Left alone, Alexandra sat at the desk, wondering who Jerome was asking on behalf of. She knew that the records office wouldn't be able to give him any information, because she was not working as a nurse, so her records wouldn't show anything. She resolved to find out why Jerome wanted to know where she was working. She got on with her work, and when the Nursing records office opened, she was able to phone them. They agreed to e-mail her details of Alexandra Louise Taylor, but told her regretfully, that she hadn't worked anywhere since leaving St. Anselm's, and was not working anywhere at the present time, which of course, she already knew.

She wrote up the report for Jerome, attached the e-mail from the Records office to it, and went into his office to take dictation. She handed him the report, and watched his face drop. "Oh blast" he said, as he read it. "He is not going to be pleased" he muttered, and Alexandra asked before she could stop herself "Who isn't going to be pleased?"
"Damien" Jerome muttered, and Alexandra looked at him. "Your brother?" she said, "Why is he not going to be pleased?" she asked again, but Jerome shook his head. "I can't give you the details Alison, I'm sorry. I'll

have to talk to Damien again, and if he ..." he broke off, and changed the subject. "Thank you for your help, Alison, now we'd better get on with the work." And he would not say anything else that wasn't connected with his patients. She was busy that day, and Jerome's words didn't stay in her head, until she remembered them later on.

When she got home that evening, she sat on the edge of the bed for a while, just thinking of the odd conversation that she had had with Jerome, and wondered again why Damien wanted to contact her, then the answer hit her. He wanted a divorce, and needed to know where she was, so that he could serve her with divorce papers! If he wanted a divorce then she would allow it, but she wanted to keep her address a secret from him. She was crying bitterly, for she knew that she still loved him, and she wanted to remain his wife, even though they were apart. "Oh Damien," she muttered. "Why did you have to have an affair? What did I do to make you want to find somebody else? I was so happy with you even when you weren't with me, and I love you so much." She lay down on the bed and sobbed, as if her heart would break, as indeed it felt as if it would. She didn't cook for herself that evening, for she didn't want to eat anything, and couldn't concentrate on anything, so she went to bed, but not to sleep, for she spent a lot of the night in tears. When she went into work the next day, her red rimmed eyes, prompted some of her friends to ask her if she was alright, for she had been unable to mask the signs of her bout of tears. "I've just had some bad news" she excused herself, and went into her office. There was a stack of audio tapes on her desk, and a

note from Jerome, asking her to get them typed as soon as possible, for they were clinic notes, and wearily, she inserted the first tape into the machine.
"Alison" she heard her name called, and looked up, to see Jerome standing in the doorway. He took one look at her face, and exclaimed "Oh my goodness. Alison, what on earth is the matter? You look absolutely tired out. You don't look as though you've slept for a week, and I think you've been crying for most of it as well. So, who's upset you?"
"I'm sorry, that's my affair" she said. "I just had some bad news that's all, but its personal to me."
"Is there anything I can do?" he asked but she shook her head. She didn't resent him asking for he was so similar to his brother, and she knew he was just trying to help her.
"I don't think you can do anything at all" she said "If there was anything I could tell you, I would, but I'm sorry, there's nothing. Now," she drew in a deep breath "What did you want me for? Is it important?"
"Not really" he muttered "Just some more dictation if you've got a few minutes to spare."
"Of course, I have" she picked up her pencil and notebook. "I'll come to your office?"
He nodded, and went into his office, and she swiftly followed him. He dictated a few letters and went to stand when he had finished, but he motioned her to stay where she was. "You've said your problems are personal, but Alison, if there's anything I can do, please would you let me know. I know you haven't worked for me for very long, but you're a very good secretary, and I like you, and we work well together. Also, I was wondering what you were doing for Christmas? Do you have any family to go to, because if you don't, perhaps

you'd like to spend it with me and my family? I don't know who'll be with us this year, but certainly my brother, my wife and hopefully my sister will be there. What do you say?"

She knew she had to refuse. "That's very kind of you" she said now, making up plans on the spot "I'll be going to spend Christmas with friends, so I don't think I'll be able to say yes, but it was kind of you to offer to have me. Will you thank your wife for me please?"

"I will Alison, and I'm sorry you won't be coming, but I hope your Christmas will be a good one." he sighed, "Now, I've got to e-mail my brother, and give him that report you got for me yesterday. I tried phoning him, but he's out of the country again and unavailable at the moment, but he's not going to be very happy at the answer."

"Does he spend a lot of time out of the country?" Alexandra asked, despite the fact that she knew the answer anyway, and Jerome nodded, "Yes, unfortunately his job means that he does. He's away from home quite frequently."

"Must be hard on his wife" she remarked, and he shook his head.

"Very hard luck, I think..." but he stopped, and said nothing more. Alexandra stood up again, "I'll get these typed for you, now, before I get on again with the clinic notes." she said, as she gathered her notes together, and walked to the door. "Thanks Alison" he muttered, as she left the office, and she made her way back to her own office, on legs that didn't really want to support her.

The following day, Jerome appeared in her office, sniffing into a handkerchief, and when he sneezed

violently while dictating a letter, she looked up. "Bless you" she said, "I take it you've got a cold?" she asked and he nodded. "Caught it off the wife, I think. She's not been too bad with hers, but I think I've got it doubled. This is going to cause some problems in theatre. I think I might have to take a couple of days off, as I can't operate while sneezing everywhere."
"Go home now, and don't spread it about then. Have some hot lemon and honey with a glass of whisky, and go to bed" Alexandra said sympathetically, then laughed, "Sorry, shouldn't be giving advice to a doctor, should I?" He laughed with her, then sneezed again. "But seriously" she said, "Go home and take some Paracetamol. That will help you get rid of it." He nodded "I think I might have to take your advice" he said, sneezing violently again. "I didn't feel too bad this morning, but since I've got here, I feel a lot worse, so I might have to stay home for a couple of days." He sneezed again, and shook his head. "Sorry Alison, I think I've left you enough work to be getting on with for a couple of days, so I hope I'll be back soon. I'll get Pandora to phone you if I'm going to be off for longer" he sneezed again, and shook his head. "I'm going." He hadn't bothered to take off his coat, and now he picked up his briefcase, and left her office. She was continuing with the work she had in hand, when Patricia came to see her. "What's up with Mr. Ellis?" she asked, and Alexandra grinned. "Man flu" she said succinctly, and the two girls laughed together, "Has he left you any work to be getting on with?" she asked, and Alexandra nodded. "I'll join you later for lunch" she said, and Patricia nodded, before going back to her own desk in the typing pool. By the time Alexandra had finished the last tape, there was still a lot of the afternoon left, and

as she didn't have any more work, she went in search of Patricia. "Would you mind if I took an hour or two off, either tonight or tomorrow?" she said. "I've finished all Mr. Ellis's work, he hasn't left me anymore to be getting on with, and he looked so ill this morning, I don't really think he'll be in tomorrow." Patricia looked at her, then glanced round the room at the other girls who were all working hard. "So not really man flu after all?" she said, with a smile. "I've got no objection if you want to take all tomorrow off, as part of your annual leave entitlement. You haven't used all you're entitled to, so if you want tomorrow off, it will suit me quite well. But Alison, are you okay? You look very tired, and I'll swear you've lost weight, and you don't seem to eat enough to keep a fly alive." Alexandra nodded and tried to reassure her friend.

"I'm okay Patricia, honestly. I've had some bad news and it's a bit worrying, but I'm sure I'll be okay, and I've been trying to lose weight anyway, so obviously my diet is doing some good."

"Why do you want to lose weight?" her supervisor demanded. "You've not got any spare flesh on you. Now if it were me" she tailed off, and Alexandra grinned, for Patricia's efforts to lose weight were well known. "I'm just a little bit heavy at the moment. I'll probably put it all back on over Christmas by eating too much"

"That's another thing. We're having the Christmas meal next week, and you haven't said whether or not you want to come?"

"Do you mind if I say no thanks? As I said, I've had some bad news recently, and I don't think I'd be very good company."

"Well, it's up to you" said Patricia, "but if you would

feel happier not coming, then we can't change your mind. You might as well go home now, and we'll see you again on Friday. Okay?" Alexandra nodded, and saying her goodbyes, left the hospital.

She walked home to the flat, got changed into a smarter outfit, and went out again. The day was coming to a close, the sky was darkening, but the shops along the high street were brightly lit, with Christmas items proliferating. She knew where she was going however, and taking a deep breath, she opened the door of the solicitor's office on the main road. She was greeted by a receptionist, who asked her business, and when she told her it was to do with a possible divorce, was able to give her an appointment for that afternoon with one of the partners. Her meeting with the solicitor was very painful for her. She had given the woman the address of Damien's flat, and stipulating that her own address was not to be given out on any account, she told her to write to him, telling him that if he wanted a divorce, he could have one, for she wouldn't object. She asked that the solicitor act as go between, saying that she did not want to meet up with him again, and the solicitor, looking at the pinched and drawn face of the woman sitting in front of her, felt sympathy for her new client. "It's not going to be a very easy divorce, unless he admits to being unfaithful" she had said. "And you'll need the name and address of the person he was unfaithful with."
"You're not listening" Alexandra argued "I don't want to divorce him, but I think he wants to divorce me. If he wants one, then he'll have to provide all that information. I've done nothing illegal, its him, who was in the wrong." She was getting angry now, for she

didn't think the solicitor had understood the complete situation. “But Mrs. Taylor-Ellis, he's quite often in the public eye, and I don't think he'll admit that he's been wrong. People in his situation won't admit that.”
“I've told you; I don't use the name Ellis. The name I’m using is Miss Alison Turner and I prefer to be addressed by that name. And I don't care that he's in the public eye. He shouldn't have committed adultery if he didn't want his name dragged through the divorce courts.” She was adamant, and the solicitor reluctantly nodded. “I'll write to him, I won't reveal your address, but I'll let you know what he says. Is that okay?” Alexandra nodded, then remembered to make sure the solicitor was aware of her alias. “When you write to me, could you please make sure you address it to Miss A. Turner. I'm using that name at work, and my landlady doesn't know my real name.” The solicitor agreed, writing it in the notes, and Alexandra stood, her tears starting to flow, dabbing her eyes as she prepared to take her departure. As she left, she couldn't help wondering how good the solicitor was, for the woman hadn't seemed to take as many notes as she thought she would take, and wondered if she were any good. She had been able to get an appointment very quickly, she thought to herself, and normally they were difficult to come by. She had left the office and walked away, deciding to have a cup of coffee, and slowly made her way along the High Street, avoiding the crowds of people who were thronging the pavement for it was late night shopping. She had stopped to look in the window of a shop, and when she turned back from it, a man cannoned into her, almost knocking her off her feet “Oh, sorry” he said, holding her steady, as she almost fell, and she looked up into his face. The man

was the living image of her husband, and she took a step back. "You're not hurt?" he asked, and she shook her head, "Excuse me please" she muttered, and almost ran away from him, only slowing as she slipped down a side street, away from the crowds. The man stood looking after her, then turned, and went on his way. Forgetting about her coffee, Alexandra walked speedily to her flat, and let herself in, but before she could take her coat off, heard Mrs. Megson calling her from downstairs. "Are you there Alison?" she asked, and on opening the door, she found her landlady standing at the foot of the stairs, looking upwards. "Yes, Mrs. M. How are you today?"
"Not so good my dear. I just wondered if you wouldn't mind coming with me to the hospital, because I don't feel at all well."
"Of course I'll come", she grabbed her handbag, and went downstairs, to assist the older lady. "I think I'll call a taxi" she said, after taking a close look at her landlady's face, surreptitiously taking her pulse, and not liking the lack of colour in the woman's face, "the journey to the hospital might be a bit difficult for you." Mrs. Megson nodded, and pointed towards the phone "There's a number in the book" she said, and Alexandra swiftly made a call. "It will be here in a few minutes" she said now. "Let's get your coat ready, so the driver doesn't have to wait for us." and she went to get the old lady ready with a small bag packed, in case she needed to stay in. Their journey to hospital was quick, for the driver took one look at his passenger and thought she looked very ill, used all the back ways to avoid the rush hour, and Mrs. Megson was swiftly taken off to be examined, when they arrived at the hospital. Alexandra went to pay for the taxi, but the

driver refused to take any money. "I thought she looked really bad, so there's no charge. Hope she's soon a lot better." Alexandra thanked him, and went back to wait for news of her landlady. The hospital decided to keep her in for a few days, and promising to come back and see her the following day, Alexandra went home for the third time. By the time she had made sure that the old lady had turned off all her electrical appliances, dealt with the cat that lived with the old lady, fed him, and gone back upstairs to her flat, she was tired, for she hadn't been sleeping very well all week, so boiled herself an egg, and after eating it went to get ready for bed. She was in bed and sitting up against her pillows, when she finally had time to think about the man who had bumped into her. If it hadn't been for the fact that he hadn't recognised her, she would have sworn that it was Damien, but it wasn't, despite the fact that he was his absolute double. Thinking about Damien, bought all her misery rushing back, and despite the fact that she knew she probably wouldn't sleep again, with all the memories rushing back into her head, she opened her phone, and turned to the photo section. The photos she had taken on their honeymoon were on it, and although there were lots of photos of scenery, she had also taken lots of photos of him. He was happy, laughing and smiling at her in the pictures, and she cried bitterly as she remembered the fantastic time they had enjoyed while they were away, before things started to change. They had made love every day, holding each other tight at night, cuddling close to each other, and she had been so very happy, to be with him, enjoying his company, thinking that he had loved her as much as she loved him. Now, she closed the photo section on her phone, and looked at the contacts list, where Damien's number was still displayed, although she had blocked all his calls to the phone, and eventually changed the SIM card, so her number was different, knowing she would have to be sensible for the future. She laid down, turned the lights off, and despite her misery, she finally slept.

The following day, as she was off duty, before going to see how Mrs. Megson was, she decided to go and pay some bills at the bank, and because it was early, and she had time to spare before visiting time, went to have a coffee. She had entered the cafe she had been heading for, the day before and sat down at a spare table, when she was greeted by the man who had almost knocked her down. She was able to take a better look this time, and knew that he was indeed the double of her husband. "Hello again" he smiled at her. "I saw you in here, and as I'm waiting for my wife, I wondered if everything was alright. I think I almost bowled you over last night, and hoped I hadn't hurt you. You looked very shocked." She smiled at him, he was so like Damien, even his voice was similar, and she couldn't be rude to him. "No, I was just a bit shocked, but I'm fine, thank you very much." He smiled at her, as he acknowledged that, said "Good. I must be a bit more careful in future", then excused himself, as the waitress came, and she ordered her drink, and watched as the man sat down at another table nearby. She couldn't believe how similar he was to Damien, and was surreptitiously looking at him when he looked up as the doorbell rang, and stood to greet a woman, and she saw with a shock, that it was the woman who she had seen Damien with, as she ran to meet him after getting from the taxi, and kissed her, and then escorted her into the hotel. "Leila, hello darling" he called, "Come and sit down." the woman came into the coffee shop, walked past Alexandra's table, kissed the man, and sat down with her husband. Alexandra's coffee was delivered, and she stirred it, as memories ran riot in her head. The man had greeted the woman with a hug and a kiss, when she had got out of the taxi and greeted him, and then she had seen them again, going into the hotel in Richmond. But she had phoned the hotel, and been told that Mr. and Mrs. Ellis were staying as guests in the hotel! It hadn't been Damien she thought triumphantly to herself. He hadn't been unfaithful to her after all, and it was probably a coincidence that a couple with the name of Ellis was staying in the hotel. But to have discovered that after she had instructed the solicitor to write to Damien telling him she wouldn't have any objection to a divorce! She sniffed back tears, as she realised that she had completely ruined any chance that she might have had of reuniting with Damien, and knew she couldn't stay in the coffee shop, as she was likely to disgrace herself at any moment. She put the money for the coffee on the table, gathered her handbag, stood up and blindly walked out of the shop. She made her way quickly back to the solicitor's office, but was informed the letter had been sent, as she had instructed. She almost ran from the main street, into the side streets, that would ultimately lead to the hospital, and instead made her way back to her flat. As she opened the door, she burst into tears, and sitting in front of the fireplace, she sobbed as if her heart would break.

At last, when the tears had dried, she washed her

face, put on a little make up, combed her hair, and made her way to the hospital, slowing her pace, as she neared it. She pinned a smile onto her face, and made her way up to the ward where Mrs. Megson was a patient. The old lady looked a lot better than she had done the night before, and the ward sister was quite happy with the old lady's state of health. "Are you a relative dear?" she asked now, but Alexandra shook her head. "I just live in her house." she replied, "and I keep an eye on her, because I know she's not been well lately. She's never mentioned any relatives, so I don't know if she's got anybody."
"She's given her daughter as her next of kin, and I wondered if that was you."
"It's not me, I'm afraid. Have you notified her daughter?" Alexandra asked, but the sister shook her head. "She didn't want her to be informed. We've acceded to that demand, as her life didn't seem to be in any danger, but if her condition should alter, then we would have to waive those demands, and let her know." she sighed. "Probably another family rift. We see plenty of those. Oh well, you go and talk to her, tell her she'll be able to go home when the doctor has decided that everything's okay, and we hope to see you again soon."
"I'll hopefully be able to pop in tomorrow during my dinner hour, if that would be alright? I only work upstairs in the offices. I'm on a day off today which is why I was able to come and see her." The ward sister nodded. "I'm sure we can stretch a point. See you again tomorrow then." and the two parted company.

Alexandra and Mrs. Megson enjoyed a long chat, and although she didn't want her daughter to know of her condition, Mrs. Megson eventually agreed to talk to her, when she was at home again. "We had an argument" she told Alexandra sadly. "I can't even remember what it was about now, something trivial probably, we were always arguing after my husband died, and I remember that she walked out, and then phoned, telling me she was going abroad and then sent me a card telling me that she'd met and married some lawyer, but didn't tell me his name. But about six months ago, she sent me a letter to tell me she's back in the country, and living in a big house near the river, quite near in fact, but I've never been there, and we haven't seen each other for a long time. She gave me the address and telephone number, and I wanted to call her, but the more I thought about it, I felt that I couldn't." She smiled sadly at Alexandra. "I think you know yourself, what it's like to argue with somebody and not want to speak to them again." Alexandra was shocked at the old woman's words. "How do you know that?" she asked but the old lady refused to tell her at that point in time. "When I come home, I'll tell you." was all she would say, and Alexandra had to be content with that.

Chapter Four

Alexandra walked into her office on Friday morning, and found several more audio tapes on her desk, and wasn't too surprised when Jerome summoned her into his office to give her dictation. She hadn't been in the office the day before, to open his post, but it was obvious that he had got into work early, and had managed to sort out some, if not all of his incoming mail.

“I hear you had the day off yesterday” he said, as she gathered together the papers he had referred to when dictating to her. She looked at him, and nodded. “Yes, I hope you didn't mind” she asked. “I had something I needed to do, and as you weren't here, I thought it would be okay.”

“I didn't mind at all” he said, “I felt lousy all day, but this morning I felt so much better, that I thought I'd come back in.”

“I'm glad your cold is a lot better” she said. She was at the door when she turned back to face him. “Incidentally, I wanted to tell you. I was walking down the High Street, and a man bumped into me, and he was absolutely identical to you. You told me that Damien Ellis is your identical twin, but the man I met could also have been a twin. They do say that everybody has a doppelganger somewhere in the world. Just a big coincidence that he should turn up in the same area as you. I'll get these typed up for you, then start on the audio tapes again.” and she turned to leave the office. Jerome stared after her, his mouth open in disbelief, then drawing out his phone, he left a message for his brother, before going to the ward to check up on his patients.

As he opened the front door of his flat on his return from the airport, Damien was greeted by Emma, who took his case from him with a smile. "Hello Mr. Damien" she said now. "Was your trip successful?"
"Yes thanks, I'm just a bit tired. I didn't get a lot of sleep after the meeting, last night, and it was impossible to sleep on the plane because of the turbulence." he answered. "Is there a lot of post?" She nodded, and handed him a large bundle of envelopes, which he looked at, as he went to the study, and unlocked the door. "Do you want tea or coffee, or a meal" the housekeeper asked before he went inside, and he answered her absently, as he looked at the pile of post in his hands. Emma left him to open his post, and went to the kitchen to make him some sandwiches and a drink. When it was ready, she loaded a tray, and took it into the study, stopping in amazement, as she took in the scene before her. Her employer was sitting at his desk, a letter open in front of him, and tears were falling down his cheeks. "Whatever is the matter sir?" she said, placing the tray on the table near the desk.
"I've just had some bad news Emma, don't worry." and he pulled out a snow-white handkerchief and wiped his eyes with it. "It's not that bad sir, it can't be" she said softly.
"Yes, it is. I had hoped that I'd be able to get Xandra back, but she's instructed her solicitors to tell me that she wants a divorce, and hopes that I'll agree to it. Everything has got to go through her solicitors

and she doesn't want to talk to me. Oh Emma, I just wish I could talk to her, one more time, to try and find out what I did and explain everything if I can."

"You sit and eat up your sandwiches and drink your coffee. Then, you go and lay down, and try and get some sleep. When you wake up, it will all seem better. I'm sure you'll be able to find her again soon, and when you wake, you'll have some good ideas. Now drink up, while its hot." and she patted his hand, and went away. Damien stared after her. She'd only been in his employment for about 6 months, but she reminded him so much of the Nanny he had shared with his brothers when he was younger. Nanny Trotter had looked after the three boys, and later on, Marie, but she'd left to have a baby when he was nearly seven, and he'd never been able to tell her how much he owed her. It was she who'd encouraged him when he'd first become interested in maths and economics, and he owed his determination to study, to Nanny Trotter. He ate the sandwiches on the plate, drank his coffee, and made his way to the bedroom he'd shared with Alexandra, where he took off his suit, put on his dressing gown, lay down, and was soon asleep and dreaming of her.

When he awoke, it was dark outside, and he could hear the phone ringing in the hallway, and he sat up against the pillows as he heard Emma's knock on the door. "Are you awake Mr. Damien?" she called, "Your brother is on the phone for you."

"Thanks Emma" he said, and swinging his legs off the bed, he went out into the hallway, to take the call.

"Hi Bro," he answered. "What can I do for you?"
"Don't you ever look at your phone messages?" his brother sounded annoyed. "I left a message for you this morning, but you've not got back to me."
"Sorry Bro" he apologised. "I only got back into the country this morning, I'd turned the phone off while on the plane, and I forgot to turn it back on. I've been asleep since I got in; What's the problem."
Jerome laughed shortly. "No problem" he said, "I've got some very big news you're going to want to hear. Unfortunately, I can't leave the hospital at the moment, so do you want to come and see me in my office, and I can let you hear my news? I don't want to give it to you over the phone, so you'll have to come and hear it for yourself."
"Okay," he answered "I'll come up to your office, and we can talk there." He ran his hand through his hair, and called "Emma". She appeared at the kitchen door and looked at him. "I've got to go out for a while, but I'll be back later on. Can dinner wait for a while?"
"Of course it can. Just give me a ring before you get home, and it'll be ready and waiting for you when you arrive." He went back to the bedroom, showered, got changed into casual clothes, and went out to the garage, to make the journey to the hospital. As he drove into the forecourt of the hospital, and parked the car, he glanced around him, for hospitals were Xandra's world, and he was not a part of it. He made his way up to the offices, deserted now, for it was long past the time when the secretarial staff had gone home, and walked into Jerome's office. His brother was sitting at his desk,

dictating into a machine, but he put down the microphone when Damien appeared, stood up and shook his brother's hand. "So, what is your big news?" Damien asked, and Jerome grinned. "I think we've got a lead on Steven's whereabouts" he announced, and Damien stared at him, shocked at his announcement. "How on earth did you manage that?" he asked, and Jerome grinned at him. "My secretary announced it after she'd taken dictation this morning. What she said was, that she'd met a man in the High Street here, she'd bumped into him, and apparently, he was the absolute image of me. She reckons that everybody has a doppelganger somewhere in the world, and she also reckons it's a coincidence that ours should turn up in this area." he grinned. "It's got to be Steven. There can't be more than one other person in this world who looks like us. We've got to try and meet up with him, and try and talk to him."

"Yes, I agree" Damien looked at his brother. "When did your secretary say that she bumped into him?"

"Yesterday, or the day before, I think." Jerome answered. "She said she was walking down the High Street and encountered him. I was going to talk to her about it, but she'd gone by the time I'd finished in theatre this afternoon. I think I ought to ask her for more information and find out exactly where on the High Street it was. You haven't met her, have you? Perhaps we could talk to her together? She'll be in on Monday, but perhaps we could go to her flat tonight, and see if she's in. I've got her address here. What do you think?"

"It would be a good idea to go now, but aren't you

needed here?"
"No, my registrar just phoned and said I wasn't needed, so as long as I've got my phone so they can contact me, I can leave the hospital. But I'll drive, just in case I need to get back here sharpish." Damien agreed, and followed him out to where his car was parked. The drive to Alexandra's flat was short and when they arrived, they were disappointed to find the house in darkness. It was obvious that nobody was in, and they walked back to the car to return to the hospital, just as Alexandra turned the corner to return to her flat. She had visited Mrs. Megson on her way home, so she was later than she usually was. She stopped short, as she saw, and with a shock, recognised her two visitors, and drew back into the shadows, and watched as they got into the car, and drove away. Thanking heaven that she had not been in, for she would have opened the door, and would have come face to face with her husband! She watched and waited while the car drove away, up the road, and turned the corner, before she went to let herself in the flat. As she shut the door behind her, she wondered why her boss and his brother had come to see her, and guessed, correctly, that it was to do with the man she had bumped into, on the High Street. She could hear Mrs. Megson's cat calling, and went into the kitchen to feed it, before going upstairs to her own flat to make herself a small meal, before showering and preparing for bed.

Damien had showed Jerome the letter he had received from Xandra's solicitors, and his brother had read it closely, but had not been able to give him any comfort. “Why don't you write to the solicitors, tell them you don't particularly want a divorce, but you would like to contact Xandra again, maybe meet up with her again, and ask them if they could arrange it? Perhaps you could write her a letter and ask them to pass it on to her. They can only say no, can't they?”

“Yes,” Damien was uncertain as to whether this would help, but now he made his mind up. “Yes, I'll definitely write, but I’ll ask them to arrange a meeting after Christmas now, because I'll be going away again shortly.” Jerome snorted. “I think I’ve got a very good idea why she left. You were never in the country, were you? How much time did you actually spend together?” Damien ignored him, and continued. “If we get any result from this thing with Steven, hopefully we can sort two things out with one letter. I still reckon that it was him, that she saw with a woman, and as we're completely identical, it’s understandable she should get confused.” he sighed, “I think your secretary needs a pay rise – thank heavens she mentioned seeing him to you.” Jerome nodded. “I told Pandora about her, and as she seems to be quite alone, we invited her for Christmas, but she said she's spending the time with friends, so she won't be able to come and stay. But I think I need to get her a decent present, just to say thank you. Any ideas?”

“What does she like?” Damien asked, but Jerome didn't know. “Ask her friends in the typing pool, if they've got any ideas, and then get her something.” Damien smiled, “Don't forget to put my name on it as well, because she might be giving me the best Christmas present of all, if we find out that it was

Steven she saw, with a woman, and I can persuade Xandra of that fact, if I can get in touch with her again. In fact, I might nip to your secretary's flat again tonight, and see if she's returned. I'll just give Emma a ring, let her know I'll be on my way soon, then at least I'll be able to have a meal in my own flat tonight. I think I'm fed up with living out of a suitcase in hotels. This last trip was so bad. I got bored, and that's saying something." he grinned again. "I've already decided that I need to rethink the way I work. Even if I don't find Xandra again, I'm going to tell the company that I'm not going to do so many foreign trips as I have been doing. They can find somebody else."

"Well, it's about time you decided that your personal life means more to you, than your job." his brother told him, and Damien agreed, pulling his phone out of his pocket to phone Emma. He made the call, laid it down on the desk, and the screen went blank, as the two brothers chatted on. "Can you pass me my phone?" he asked, after a while, and Jerome handed it to him, as he stood to leave, so that he didn't see the screen saver picture, which had been taken on their honeymoon, and was of Alexandra laughing at the camera. They said their goodbyes, Jerome went back to the office to finish his dictation, before going home, and Damien went out to the car park, to retrieve his car and drive to the flat again. Alexandra had turned off the lights in the front room, before going to have a shower, so the house appeared to still be in darkness. He took out his notebook, and wrote a short note, explaining why he was interested in talking to her, asking if she could phone him during the weekend, made sure the phone number was correct, posted it through the letter box, and went back to his flat.

When Alexandra went downstairs the following morning to feed the cat, she found Damien's note on the doormat, and she burst into tears again, at the sight of his well-loved and well-remembered handwriting. She read it, and wondered whether or not to phone him, because she was sure he would recognise her voice, and she did not want him to do that. Instead, she fed the cat, and allowed him to go outside, waiting for him to come back inside, and then decided that if a Mr. Ellis wanted to talk to her, she would phone Jerome instead. She could always say that she had only glanced at the note, seen the surname Ellis, and assumed it was her boss, calling her. She was not to know that Damien had been persuaded by Jerome, to spend some of the weekend with him, so later that morning, she phoned Jerome, and asked him why he had visited her flat the previous evening. "I thought I'd told you what I saw?" she said, and Jerome, who had put the phone onto speaker, motioned to his brother to come and listen. "Yes, you did, and I'm sorry to bother you again, Alison," he said. "But my brother and I just wanted to know exactly where you saw the man you described as my double. My brother is with me, incidentally, listening to everything you say."
"Oh," Alexandra sighed, and wondered what Damien would say if she told him who she was. "I met the man twice." she answered. "The first time was on

Wednesday evening, when I was in the High Street, near Marks and Spencer. I'd stopped to look in the window of Jacksons, the stationers, and as I turned around, we collided, and the second time, was on Thursday lunchtime. I was in the coffee shop, so was he, and he came to speak to me, said he hoped he hadn't hurt me when he bumped into me the night before, told me he was waiting for his wife, and when she came in, he called her Leila. She was very glamorous, looked as if she could have been a model. But that was all the conversation I had with him."

"That's very helpful Alison, thanks very much. Whereabouts is the coffee shop?"

She told him the name of the shop, gave its whereabouts, and prepared to disconnect, when her curiosity piqued, she asked. "Why do you want to talk to him? Just because he looks like you, or is there another reason?" Jerome sighed, and knew he would have to explain things to her. "We've got another brother, Steven, who we haven't spoken to for many years, and we'd like to try and find this man who might be him, and he might be able to help us the other person we've been trying to find, the woman who you asked about, in the nursing records – Alexandra Louise Taylor. She seems to have disappeared completely. Alison, what would you do if you were trying to hide from somebody?"

"I'd change my name, alter my appearance and move away." she said promptly, then hesitated, "You must want to find this woman pretty badly?" she questioned, and looked at her reflection in the mirror, wondering what he would say. "It's Damien who wants to find her." he said, but nothing more,

"Anyway, see you on Monday."
"You too." she agreed. "Enjoy your weekend." and at his laconic "Thanks", she disconnected. Why did Damien want to find her so badly she wondered. Unless it was to deliver the divorce papers to her by hand, but he would have received a letter from the solicitors, and knew he could just make sure that they delivered them to her. She got ready to go out, and went to the local shops to buy her food for the weekend, hoping that they wouldn't think of trying to find Steven until after the weekend. She bought enough food for Mrs. Megson as well, for she knew that the woman would probably be discharged on Monday, and knew she wouldn't have the opportunity to shop for her then, for she would be at work during the day. She missed the old woman, so that afternoon, she went back to the hospital, to visit her, and spent a while, just chatting about generalities. Before she left however, the old woman took her hand, and squeezed it tight. "Alison, I know you've got problems at the moment, and you're not happy. I also know you've got no relatives to talk to, so if you ever need to talk to someone, or get some advice from, then you know I'd be only too willing to listen, and perhaps help. I'm not a gossip, I promise I won't tell anybody any of your dark secrets, but the offer is there if you need it." Alexandra was overwhelmed by the kind offer, and knew that here was the person she could talk to. "I might take you up on that offer when you get home" she said "As you say, I do want to talk to somebody, because I don't know what to do about a situation, I find myself in, so I'd love to talk to you,

and get your advice." she sighed. "I don't know what I'm going to do." Mrs. Megson patted her hand. "When I get home, we'll have a chat" she declared, and Alexandra smiled at her. "I'll look forward to it. Now, do you want anything special got in for you, when you get home?" The old woman refused her offer, and Alexandra said her farewells, and left the ward.

That evening, she sat in her flat, just staring at the television – there was nothing she wanted to watch, just wanted some noise in the background, and wondered about her conversation with Jerome that morning. Steven Ellis, she mused. It must have been him she had seen with his wife, her brother-in-law, she admitted to herself, and wished she could speak to Damien and tell him that she had been mistaken, but she had burnt her boats when she walked out on him. She wanted to tell him she was sorry, but now she knew he wanted to know where she lived, so he could serve divorce papers on her, she didn't think he'd ever want to talk to her again. She turned off the television, made herself a cup of tea and took it into the bedroom to drink, while she prepared for bed crying bitter tears as she did so.

The following day, she went to her local church for the morning service, before going for a walk along the banks of the Thames, and admired the large houses, with their grounds sweeping down to the river, before going back to the hospital to visit Mrs. Megson. The old lady took one look at her, and sat up straight. "You've been crying again" she stated. "And I know you've lost more weight recently. You've got to eat more than you do at present, because you'll be ill if you don't." Alexandra looked at her, as she sat down. "I don't want to eat" she declared "I've done something very stupid, but I did have a reason, and its consequences are worrying me. And yes, I have been crying, but I'm alright really."

"Well, you don't look alright" the old lady said vehemently, and Alexandra laughed suddenly. "You're feeling better" she declared. "You must be, if you're telling me off."

"What did you have for lunch?" her landlady asked, but Alexandra shook her head. "I didn't have any. I'll have something later on."

"Oh Alison. You've got to eat properly. You've lost so much weight since you started living with me. And in the past few weeks you've lost even more. You're not sleeping properly either, I'll bet. Why don't you go home, lie down, and try and get some sleep this afternoon?"

"Because I'm visiting you" she declared, but Mrs. Megson shook her head. "You need some sleep before you become ill. Go home, have a meal and have an early night. Don't worry about me, I'll be home tomorrow afternoon. I can get a taxi home, and Sister says I won't be leaving until after lunch anyway, and then when you come home from work, you and I are going to have a long chat. I'm not going to ask you to talk now, because I don't think you'd fancy having hysterics in the middle of the ward, and we can't guarantee that we'd be left in peace, so we'll talk tomorrow evening. Just the two of us, with nobody to interrupt us. And there's going to be no refusing either. You need help, and I'm going to be able to give it to you." And Alexandra knew she meant what she said. After a while, she said goodbye to the old lady, and went home. She fed the cat, cooked herself a small meal, and then suddenly feeling very tired, went to bed and managed to sleep for almost all of the night.

The following day, Jerome said nothing to her, about their telephone conversation on Saturday, and she didn't want to raise the subject with him, so got on with her work, and hoped that he wouldn't say anything before she had managed to have a talk with Mrs. Megson. She hoped the old lady would be able to help her, and resolved to tell her everything, about her marriage, the mistake she had made with her identification of Damien and Steven, and the problems she was now experiencing. By the time she was able to go home, she was on edge, and very short with some of her colleagues. Patricia came into her office and took a long look at her as she put her coat on. "Alison, if you're having problems, try and sort them out, and don't bring them into work. I know it's not easy, but you're going to alienate everybody if you carry on like this." Alexandra nodded at her supervisor's words. "I know Patricia. I'm sorry, I don't mean to bring my troubles into work, and hopefully, I'll be talking to somebody tonight who'll be able to give me some help. I'll try harder, I promise." she caught up her handbag, "I'll see you tomorrow. Okay?" and at her friends' nod, she walked out of the office to go home.

That evening, she had cooked a meal for them both, cheese and tomato omelettes, and made a pot of tea which she shared with Mrs. Megson, before she sat down with the old lady, to have a chat. “Talk” the woman commanded, “and don't leave anything out. I want to know it all, because if you don't tell me everything, I won't be able to help you. So, what's worrying you, Alison?”
Alexandra knew she was going to have to tell the old lady everything, so took a deep breath, and began to talk. “To start” she said, “My name isn't Alison Turner, my real name is Alexandra Taylor-Ellis. I got married nearly 19 months ago, to the most wonderful man in the world, Damien Ellis.” She was concentrating on what she was saying, and didn’t see the old lady stiffen and look at her with shock. “We had a great time at the start of our married life, I was very happy with him, but gradually his work got busier, and he would have to go abroad for days at a time, and when he was in the country, he'd frequently be late home from the office, so we didn't manage to get out and about very often. But when we were together, our life was marvellous, and I thought he loved me, as much as I love him. But I was bored. I had absolutely nothing to do. The housekeeper he had, was a really nasty woman, obviously didn't like me, but when he and I were together before I gave up work, I didn't realise how nasty she was. When we got back from our honeymoon, and I was at home all day, I found out. She didn’t allow me to do anything in the flat we lived in, she did all the cooking and cleaning, leaving

me with nothing at all to do, and she made me feel as if I were an intruder. I'd washed out some smalls one evening, put them to dry in the ensuite bathroom, and the following morning, I looked for them, and she'd put them in the washing machine and washed them again! I couldn't even do any of my own washing! She didn't like me staying in the flat during the day, made it quite clear, by asking me when I was going to go out, and I couldn't argue with her, so I'd go out for the day. As I said, I was bored, and there's a limit to the number of books you can read, or the times you can go shopping. All of my friends seemed to desert me, didn't want to stay in contact, and I was very lonely. My husband gave me a good clothes allowance, so I didn't want for anything, but I wanted to do something, to occupy my time. We'd been married nearly eight months, and the situation was getting worse and worse, so when I found that I could do some voluntary work in an orphanage near our home, I was overjoyed. When I told Damien what I was going to do, he asked me not to, as doing something like that would tie me down, and if there was a chance we could just go off for a few days, then I probably wouldn't be able to make it. I did tell him that it was voluntary, and I wouldn't be tied down to regular hours, but he didn't seem to listen to me." she drew in a deep breath, and Mrs. Megson who had been listening intently, patted her hand. "Go on dear" she said now. "You'll feel better once you've told somebody." Alexandra nodded and continued. "Anyway, after that, he didn't take me away, he never seemed to be at home, or when he was home, he'd spend the evenings in his study, so we didn't even talk. If we did manage to have a conversation, he never seemed to listen to what I was saying, so in the end I stopped trying. I worked it out one day, after I'd left him, and in the eleven months we'd been married, he'd been away or abroad for six of them. Six months! He'd spent more time abroad, than with me! Was it any wonder I was fed up?" she asked rhetorically, and Mrs. Megson nodded her head wisely, but let her continue speaking.

"Anyway, one night soon after that, he'd just come back from a foreign trip, he didn't go to his study, and we were able to spend the evening together, I asked him why he couldn't spend more time with me, and he said he was incredibly busy. I said something like, oh too busy to be with me then, and we had a big row. We made it up that night, but the next morning, he told me he wouldn't be home that night, as he had to be available for a high-level conference, and would be staying in a hotel because it might finish very late, and there was a possibility that he would be very late home the day after, because he was going to be involved in serious meetings with some foreign investors, then he kissed me goodbye and left. The housekeeper came in then, wanted to know what time I was going out, and it was obvious she just wanted to me to leave her alone in the flat. So, I went shopping – again. I was in Oxford Street, and looking at clothes in the window of John Lewis, when I saw this incredibly good looking, very well dressed, woman get out of a taxi, and there running towards her, I saw Damien. She flew into his arms, he held her close, kissed her, and they got into the taxi together and drove away. I was so shocked, I couldn't have said anything to him at that point, so I just went home, wanting to have a chat with him, but of course he wasn't there. I wanted to phone him, to talk to him and ask him to explain, but he'd told me never to do so unless it was life or death, but the way I felt, it was. I did phone, but his secretary said he wasn't available, but she'd tell him I'd phoned, and she'd ask him to phone me. But he didn't contact me, either then or the following day. So, the next day, I knew I'd have to have a talk with him, but I'd got to wait all day for him to come home. The old witch wanted to know when I was going out again, so because I didn't want to go shopping again, I went out for a long walk in Richmond Park, to try and do something to pass the time. I was on the verge of going home, when saw Damien and the woman going up the stairs of the hotel opposite it. When I got home, I phoned the hotel and was told that Mr. & Mrs. Ellis were guests of the hotel. The receptionist asked me if I wanted to speak to them, and when the phone was picked up, I heard Damien say 'hang on darling' then he said 'hello', but I found I couldn't speak, and put the phone down. I knew then that he'd found somebody else, he didn't love me, and I knew I couldn't stay with him any longer. I packed my clothes, found your flat, and left Damien. I haven't had any contact with him since then. But last week, I was in the High Street, and I bumped into a man who was the absolute double of him, and the following day, I saw him again, and he was with his wife, who was the woman I'd seen run into his arms outside John Lewis. Trouble is, the day before I saw him, I'd been to see a solicitor, who'd written to Damien, telling him I wouldn't contest it, if he wanted a divorce, and it was only then I realised that it hadn't been Damien, it had been this other man. The solicitors said they'd written to him already, and the letter had already been posted. So, I've spoilt everything, and now, I don't know what to do." and she burst into tears, and sobbed as if her heart would break.

Chapter Five

Mrs. Megson let her cry for a few minutes, before she spoke. "Why don't you phone him and tell him you made a mistake?" she asked but Alexandra shook her head. "I can't." she said simply. "I want to, but telling him that I had, would make it seem that I just want to go back to how we were, and I don't want to do that. Yes, I love him, but I don't think I can just go and continue to live how we did before I left him. He was never at home, and I was so lonely, and I don't want to go back to living like that again. His job is important to him, and he's good at it. The trouble is, I told you that my boss at the hospital left a couple of months ago? Well, the man who has been appointed to replace him, is my husband's brother. It's bad enough not being able to see Damien again, but I have to work with somebody who is his identical twin. In actual fact, he's not quite identical, because his hair is lighter, and he's got a bit of grey in it, and Damien's hair is still really dark brown from what I've seen when he was on television recently. But I told my boss about the other man I'd seen, and now he and Damien want to find this other man. When I asked why, Jerome, that's my boss, told me that they had another brother, but they'd lost touch, and they want to contact him, to see if it is him. I went to a Christmas party at Jerome's house, because he'd said that Damien wasn't going to be there, and we were all wearing masks, so nobody could see my face, but when Damien suddenly arrived, I left, because we were all going to take our masks off at midnight, and

I didn't want him to see me again, so I left without talking to him. I wish I'd been able to, but I couldn't make myself. But there's another thing. Jerome asked me, after the party, if I'd be able to do something for him, and find out if a woman called Alexandra Louise Taylor was working as a nurse, and if so, where. He said that somebody wants to contact her, and I reckon that it's Damien, and all he wants is a divorce, and needs to know where he can send the papers. So, perhaps you can understand why I'm so unhappy at the moment. I still love Damien, but if he wants a divorce, then I'll have to try and forget about him. That's why I got my solicitors to send him a letter telling him, that I wouldn't object if he wanted to divorce me. And then I saw the man who looks like him, and he was with his wife, and I don't think Damien was unfaithful to me after all." and she started to cry again.

"Oh Alison, or would you prefer me to call you Alexandra? I don't know what to suggest. But I think I'd better tell you now, I know the family very well. I was nanny to the boys, Damien, Jerome and Steven, and then their sister Maria, before I left when the boys were nearly seven years old, because I was pregnant with my daughter. However," she said, holding Alexandra's hand, as she tried to pull away, "I haven't been in touch with any of them, since I left. They were little imps then, but it sounds as if they've all settled down now. Damien was the first baby, by 10 minutes, he was always the studious one, he loved numbers then, and it sounds as if he's done well for himself. Jerome was the youngest baby, even when he was so young, he always wanted to be a doctor – their father was one you know, but Steven was Damien's identical twin, and he was a little tearaway. He wouldn't settle down, no matter what I tried. He was always the adventurous one but very secretive, kept himself to himself, and didn't talk very much. He was my failure, if you can call it that. I've occasionally seen pictures of Damien and Jerome in the papers, and tried to keep up to date with them that way, but I didn't know all about their problems. But why hasn't Jerome told Damien that you're working with him? He would have told him that he was working with you now because Damien would have told his brother he wanted to find you."

"Because I changed my name and never told anybody my real one, so Jerome has no idea that his secretary is also his sister-in-law. I also tried to alter my appearance, so I've dyed my hair a different colour, just in case Jerome knows that his sister-in-law is a blue eyed blonde."

"How did you and Damien meet anyway?" Mrs. Megson queried, and Alexandra smiled as she remembered. "Well, before we married, I was a Staff Nurse on a surgical ward." Alexandra replied. "He was admitted to the ward I was working on at St. Anselm's to have his appendix removed, and I nursed him. We married six weeks later. Because we hadn't been together too long, and I was still working, I didn't realise what living with him, in his flat, would be like, so I was quite unprepared when we came back from our honeymoon, and found out what his housekeeper was really like. When I left him, I decided not to go back to working as a nurse, but instead got a job as a secretary, in St Catherine's" and she named the hospital where Mrs. Megson had recently been a patient. "I was lucky, I did secretarial qualifications at school, before I did my nurse training. At least I've got other skills to be able to earn a living."

"Didn't you ever meet any of the family when you were married? Damien and Jerome were always so close, I can't think he'd have wanted to keep you a secret from everybody."

"No, we got married in a very small ceremony. We only had one of Damien's friends, and my best friend from the hospital as witnesses. Damien said his brother was abroad at the time. And after we were married, when we had arranged to meet up with other members of the family, Damien had to go away, out of the country, the meeting was cancelled, and we never managed it. And Jerome only got back to this country about 5 or 6 months ago, apparently. Damien never told me that his brother was in fact, his identical twin, or for that matter, that he was one of a set of triplets. He'd told me he was part of a large family, but never mentioned anything like that, and he didn't have any photos of his family on display."

Mrs. Megson shook her head sadly. "Oh dear," she said, "Damien always liked to spring surprises on people, but I think that one has misfired." She hesitated, then, "You once told me that your parents had died. When did that happen? And you also mentioned you were bought up a children's home, but when did they pass away, and how old were you when they died?"

"I was 14. They'd been out for the day to visit friends who I didn't like very much, because of the way they

treated me. Mum knew how I felt, and as I had some exams to take, I persuaded her to let me stay at home to revise. My parents were killed in a car crash on their way home. I was taken to the children's home about two days later and stayed there for the next four years. I remember being taken to their funeral, and feeling so lonely that they'd gone, and realising I'd never be able to talk to them again. I was crying afterwards, and remember being comforted by one of the workers there." she sighed, "I didn't take the exams I'd been revising for either, and after everything, I went to a different school, so I had to concentrate on being able to earn a living when I left, which is why I did secretarial training, while I was waiting to start training."
"You've not had it too easy have you my dear?"
"No, but I don't pity myself" she said now. "I've got a good job, I'm lucky to be living in your flat, and although I don't have many friends now, I'm okay. I just wish I could sort out what to do about Damien. Jerome keeps on telling me that he wants me to meet up with his brother, and even invited me to stay at his home over Christmas, but I refused, when he told me his brother was going to be there. You can probably understand why?" she smiled tearfully, and the old lady nodded. "Let me have a good think about what we can do" she said now. "I'm sure we can sort out your problems, if we put our heads together. But in the meantime, you just carry on with your work at the hospital, and I'll see if I can think of something. Did you mean it dear? You'd like to get back together with Damien, but only if he changes his way of life?" Alexandra nodded. "I still

love him" she declared. "I didn't want to have to go in the first place, but as I thought he was having an affair, and he looked so happy when he met up with that other woman, I didn't see how I was going to be able to carry on. But now I know, it wasn't him at all, but that other man, Steven and the woman he met is his wife, well, you can see how difficult it would be."
"I can indeed my dear. Now, let's have another cup of tea, if you wouldn't mind putting the kettle on, then you can have an early night, and get some sleep."

The following morning, Alexandra went into work feeling better for having told her landlady all about her problems, and hoping that the old woman would have some good ideas of what to do. She had slept better than she had done for a long time, despite her tears that evening, and she felt rested. Jerome obviously thought so, for he took a long look at her face, as she went into his office to take dictation.
"You look as though you've slept properly" he remarked. "Have you managed to sort out your personal problems now?"
"Not quite" she said, "but I've had a long talk with somebody, and she is going to help me, if she can, so I feel a lot better now thank you."
"More than I do" he replied gloomily. "I can't find anybody who knows where that brother of mine is living, if it is him, and now Damien's had to go abroad again for a while, so I'm going to have to do this all on my own. Pandora can't help me, because she's just been asked to do some photographic work and is going to be working practically every day until just

before the holiday, and I don't want to have to leave it until after Christmas. We've been estranged for so long now; I just want us to get back together. I can't see that this Christmas is going to be much fun at all. Pandora's mother won't be with us, because she's going to stay with her sister, I don't think Damien will be able to be with us now, so it's going to be quiet."
She sympathised, wondering why Damien would be absent from a family Christmas, but not wanting to ask. She gathered up her papers and prepared to go, when he asked where she was going for the holidays.
"I'm staying with friends who live quite near here" she answered, for that was the first thing that came into her head. "Why do you ask?"
"Well, I wondered if you wanted to come and see us over the festive period" he answered, "I know you're staying with friends, but if you got fed up, you could come and meet Pandora and my sister, and maybe, if he ever gets back, Damien, as well."
"That's very kind of you to offer, but I don't think I'll have the time. I think my friends have got a lot of things they want us to do, because we don't see each other very often, so we have a lot of things to catch up on. But I'll keep the offer in mind, and if we get to a stage where we can't stand each other's company, then I might phone you and see if you're in." she smiled, as she went to the door, only to spin round and face him when he asked suddenly, "Why did you phone me on Saturday morning? Damien said he left a note through the door, giving his phone number, but when you phoned, you phoned me, instead of him and I was just wondering why?"
"I" she stuttered, then recalled her thought on

Saturday morning. “I just saw the name Ellis, thought it had to be you, so I phoned you. I didn't realise until afterwards, that it was a different name and phone number on the note. Sorry”
“No problem” he said, “Damien reckoned that was what it was” and breathing a sigh of relief, she left his office. Jerome stared after her. She was definitely hiding something, he thought and wondered what it could be.

Alexandra sat at her desk, her fingers busy on the keyboard, but her mind racing after her conversation with Jerome. If Damien were going to be abroad for a while, she might be able to meet up with Emma again, and wondered if she dared phone the flat. She resolved to do so, for she wanted to meet up with Emma again, and see how she was.

She had just returned from her lunch break, when Patricia came into see her, and sat down on the desk. “What's the problem?” Alexandra asked, wondering what the other girl wanted to say. “It’s a bit awkward really.” the woman said. “Not for you, for me. I've just been talking to Personnel, and they've told me that you've got a lot of annual leave left to take, and I realised you haven't booked any at all. You've got to take it before the end of March, and unfortunately, some of the other girls have booked their time off then, so your options are a bit limited. I wondered if you'd like to have a couple of weeks after Christmas, and one more week and a couple of days extra in February. I'm sorry to break it up like that, but those are the only weeks that are available.

Do you think that would suit you, or would you like to be paid instead? They don't really want to do that, because they're trying to save money, so they'd like you to take the leave. They've been a bit shirty with me, because I didn't push you to have some leave earlier on this year."

"Oh Patricia, I'm sorry. I didn't really think about it. Holidays have not been very high on my agenda lately. I'll take the leave when you want me to. When would you suggest?"

"Well," the supervisor drew out a big diary, and the two girls went over the dates. "I'll talk to Mr. Ellis, and see if these dates suit him" Patricia said now, "but if it's okay, then you can come back to work after New Year, work for a week, have two weeks off, then work another three weeks, and have the rest of your leave then. I'm sorry to ask you to have time off at such an inconvenient time, and I promise you can have your pick of the time next year, as long as you decide soon, before everybody else gets their requests in for time off."

"I don't have any special requests for leave" Alexandra said sadly, "I'm not going to go away anywhere, with anybody, so I'll fit in with everybody else. Just let me know when you want me to have it, and I'll fit in with you." Patricia took a long look at her.

"Don't tell me you don't have a boyfriend, or somebody special. Somebody as pretty as you, you could take your pick of the men."

"I don't want to take my pick" she answered. "I had somebody, but I think he's found somebody else, and doesn't want me, so I'm not going to try again."

she stared down at the desk, her eyes filling with tears, and Patricia gave her a hug. "I knew there was something wrong. If you ever need to talk, or if there's anything I can do to help you, then you know I'll be here for you."

"Thanks" said Alexandra, "but I don't think anything will help. But thanks for the offer. And now," she wiped her eyes, "I'd better get on with these for Mr. Ellis, before he decides he doesn't want me to work with him again."

"That's not going to happen" said Jerome from the doorway. "She's too good to want to get rid of, Patricia. I want her to stay with me for as long as she wants to." Patricia smiled as she left the office, leaving Jerome with Alexandra. "Thank you" she said softly. "I've nearly finished these. Do you have anything else you need me to do?"

"I'd like you to be happier than you are at the moment, but these are some clinic notes I need typing. I just thought I'd better leave these with you." and he handed over a stack of tapes. "If you can get them typed for me, I'd be grateful. However," he continued, and she looked at him, "I do have a business proposition for you. I've just heard Patricia talking to you about taking some leave, and I wondered what you were going to do with your time off?"

"I haven't had much time to decide, she's only just asked me if I'd like to take time off, and said she'd talk to you about it." he nodded before speaking again.

"Yes, that's what I overheard. I'm quite amenable to being given somebody else to work for me, while you're away, but if you're not going to go anywhere, I wondered if you'd do some work for me. Well, not for me, but for my brother. He's been asked if he would be able to start some work on some high financial book, and he's made some notes and tapes, but needs to get them typed up. I wondered if you'd like to do them for him? He'd pay you obviously, for the time it would take. He wouldn't be around all the time, as I said, he's often out of the country for days on end, but if you could type a couple of tapes for him, I think he'd be grateful."

"But what about his own secretary?" she asked, "Doesn't he have somebody else who could do it?"

"Yes, he's got a secretary, but she's going off on maternity leave, so he's going to have to have somebody new to do her work, and typing a book on top of that, would obviously be an extra strain, so I said I'd ask you if you could do it."

"I wouldn't be able to get started until after Christmas" she said, knowing she wanted to do some work for Damien, and hear his voice, even if it were only dictating notes, but Jerome nodded. "I gathered that, and I'm sure it would be okay. I'll get him to give me the first couple of tapes, so if you wanted to have a listen to what you'd be doing, I'll be able to pass them onto you."

"Would it be okay if I did them at home?" she asked and he nodded. "I don't think you'd want to go to his flat to work, as he's frequently not there and his office is in the middle of Whitehall, and not easy to get to, and you'd need special clearance to be able to get into it, so if you worked at home, then you'd be able to take time off whenever you needed to. You

could just charge him for the hours you worked."
"I'm quite amenable to working for him" she said now, thanking heaven she would not be expected to go to the flat or his office, "Let me have the tapes when you can, and I'll get going on them when I'm off. I'll be working for a week after Christmas, then taking two weeks off. If your brother wants to leave any more tapes with you, then you could pass them on when I'm here. How long is he going to be away anyway?" she asked, wondering if Jerome would sense her interest, but he said nothing, "Oh, he's been asked to go and stay with some people in the Far East, and he reckons that he'll be away for the next fortnight at least. Honestly, what a job. He's never in the country lately. But it's good that he's got his job to take his mind off everything that's happening at the moment. He's not a happy lad at the moment either." he grinned at her mischievously and made a suggestion, "Maybe you two should to get together, then you could both be unhappy together. He's a nice man, even if I am biased, because he's, my brother."
"Yes, he sounds nice, but I don't want to get involved again" she said, looking down at the papers on her desk. Jerome shot her a swift glance. "So, it's not all men you don't like then?" he asked and she looked at him. "What do you mean?" she asked sharply, and he smiled at her. "I just made a comment that's all." he said, and she thought she was getting a bit paranoid. "Is there any rush to get your book tapes done, and do you want them saved on the computer like I did with the others?"
"Just get the clinic notes done if you wouldn't mind,

but the book tapes aren't very urgent. If you can save them, they can be printed off later on." He smiled at her again, as he walked out of Alexandra's office. "I'll let you have Damien's tapes as soon as I can. If anybody wants me, I'll be in theatre" he told her, and left the office.

That evening, she went downstairs to see Mrs. Megson, and the old lady looked very happy as she opened the door. "Hello dear, how do you feel today?" she asked, and Alexandra smiled. "I should be the one asking that." she replied, as she went in to the front room. "I'm okay, but how are you feeling today? Do you feel any better?"
"I'm fine dear. But I've got some news. You remember you told me that I ought to contact my daughter? Well, this afternoon, I plucked up courage and phoned her, and she's going to come and see me tomorrow afternoon. Hopefully, we'll be able to start talking again, and maybe she and I can put our differences behind us, and we can get back together. I miss her you know. I wish I knew what I'd done to upset her."
"You'll be able to ask her, won't you?" said Alexandra. "I'm sure it's nothing too terrible, and you'll be able to spend lots of time with her, and her husband, catching up on the past few years."
"And what about you my dear? Sit down and have a cup of tea with me, and we can have a think about what we're going to do about your problems." Alexandra went and made the old lady a pot of tea, and when it was brewed, sat with her, drinking a cup. "I don't think there's anything else I can do at the

moment" she answered. "I had a conversation with Jerome this afternoon, and he gave me some information. He told me that Damien's out of the country probably for the next two weeks, he's going to stay with some people in the Far East, so I've probably got a couple of weeks leeway before I have to think properly what I'm going to do. I haven't heard from my solicitors, so he obviously hasn't written to them yet, and as its Christmas at the end of the week, I don't think they'll be hearing from him until afterwards, so I'll be able to have Christmas without worrying what he's going to do. And afterwards, I've been asked by Jerome, if I wouldn't mind using some of my annual leave to type up some notes that Damien has made, for a book he's writing. Said he's going to pay me as well, so that's going to be some extra income."

"I meant to ask you my dear, what are you going to do for Christmas. You can't stay here on your own, and I'll be spending it with a friend. Would you like me to ask her if you can come too?"

"No thanks Mrs. Megson. I'll be going to a friend," she lied quickly, "so I'll be alright, and I'll be here when you get back. You never know, you might be asked to go and stay with your daughter." and she turned the conversation back to the meeting the next day. When she left the old lady to go back upstairs, she felt happy for the woman, and a little bit better herself. As she looked at her photos on her phone that evening, she wondered what Damien was doing at the moment, and when he would be leaving the country to go abroad. She resolved to phone Emma later on, and see when it would be convenient for them to meet up again.

She managed to contact Emma the following day, telling her that she was back, and asking when they could meet. “Well, dear, my employers gone away, and he's not going to be back for a fortnight at least, I'm going to see friends, so perhaps we could meet sometime after Boxing Day. You could come here if you wanted to, or perhaps you'd like to meet for coffee somewhere?”
“That would be nice” Alexandra answered her. They arranged to meet up in a coffee shop, on the day after Boxing Day. Emma had suggested meeting at the flat, but she didn't want to return to a place where she had lived with Damien, for it held too many memories for her, and as she made her way home that evening, reflected that she was lucky to have met up with somebody as nice as Emma. She bought the lady a small present – a glove and scarf set, and wrapped it nicely in Christmas paper, wrapping Mrs. Megson's present at the same time, for she had bought the old lady a lovely warm dressing gown, having seen that the one she had, was a bit threadbare, and that evening, she took it downstairs. The old lady was full of her daughters visit. They had talked, she said, and she had been invited to spend a couple of days with her daughter and her husband, just to get to know him, and catch up on what had happened since they separated, and she had accepted. “They wanted me to go and spend Christmas with them but I've already arranged that I'll be going to spend it with an old friend, so I'm going afterwards and spending a few days between

Christmas and New Year. So, you'll be here on your own after Christmas" she said now. "Will you be alright on your own? And Alison, I wondered if you'd mind keeping an eye out for the cat, and feed him for me?" Alexandra had nodded. "I'll be fine" she said. "You go and enjoy yourself with your daughter, have a lovely time, and don't worry about me or the cat." and the old lady had accepted her present, and handed over a small wrapped box of her own. "It's only a little something, but I always liked it, and I hope you will enjoy it too." she said and Alexandra had gone upstairs to her flat, placing the little box on the television table, before going to bed.

Christmas Eve arrived, and very little work got done in the hospital secretarial pool. Secret Santa gifts were exchanged in the typing pool and with the other secretaries, and Alexandra prepared to leave early, along with her colleagues. She was stopped however, by Jerome, who came into her office, as she was putting her coat on. "I'm sorry Alison" he said, "I meant to be here earlier, but I got held up. This is just a little gift from me, but it's also from Damien, to say thank you for giving us the best lead to finding Steven, we've had for a long time." and he handed over a heavy box, wrapped in gaily coloured paper. "Don't open it now" he said, "but I hope it will be suitable for you" She thanked him, wondering what it was. "Before I forget, here are Damien's tapes" and he handed over a folder. "Enjoy your Christmas, and don't forget, if you want to come and have a drink or a meal, any time over the holiday, just give us a ring. I'll see you after the holiday." He would have said more, but her phone rang, and she answered it. It was theatres, wanting to know if he was with her, so she handed him the receiver and watched as he listened to the person on the other end. “I've got to go.” he said, as he replaced the receiver. “See you soon. Have a Happy Christmas” he kissed her on the cheek, and was soon gone. She smiled, as she watched him go, for he was so like Damien in his mannerisms, and she did like working for him. She picked up her parcels, and her handbag, and left the hospital.

Chapter Six

Alexandra's Christmas was extremely quiet. Mrs. Megson had gone to stay with her friend on Christmas Eve, and she had the house to herself, for her landlady had taken the cat with her. She spent Christmas Day very quietly on her own, she had gone to church in the morning, happy to be able to sing carols with other people in the congregation, and take part in the worship, before going home to the flat. She had made an effort and cooked herself a simple dinner, and although she wasn't hungry, she had eaten it, unwilling to have to throw it away. She had listened to the radio in the morning, as she cooked her meal, and watched the Queen's speech on television after lunch, before she remembered the previous year, and how happy she and Damien had been. The housekeeper had gone away on holiday, and she had been happy just to spend the time alone with him, looking after him, cooking his meals, and they had spent the time together, very quietly with no parties or receptions. On Christmas morning, she had awoken, held in his arms, and she had been so happy, before he had given her, the presents he had for her. She had unwrapped the small box he had given her, and found it contained a sapphire and diamond necklace in an unusual setting and earrings to match. She had been overjoyed to receive them, and even more so, when Damien had told her he had designed them himself. She had loved them, but as they very rarely went out after that, she had not worn them often, and had left them behind when she left him. She had bought him a watch – a thin Rolex with a gold strap, and he had immediately put it on, and had worn it nearly all the time they had been together, and now she reflected, when she had seen him on the television, he had still been wearing it. They had spent seven glorious days together, until the holidays had come to an end, the housekeeper had returned, Damien had been asked to go abroad for a day or two, and things had gone back to how they usually were. She sighed, then went to get the Christmas presents, given to her by Jerome and by Mrs. Megson, and sat and opened them. Mrs. Megson had given her a brooch – a splendid affair of blue and white stones, in the shape of an A. It sparkled in the light, and she turned it to and fro, watching the light glimmer on the stones. It was too nice to put away, and she decided there and then to wear it. It would look lovely on her coat, she thought, and pinned it onto the lapel, where it sparkled in the light. Next, she opened the present given to her by Jerome, and found a large gift box containing make up and brushes, along with a bottle of perfume. It was the same perfume that Damien had bought her when they first got married, and she knew it suited her. It was a splendid present, she thought, and wondered who had chosen it. She didn't think that Jerome would have done so, Damien had been out of the country, so it must have been Pandora. She had never met the woman, but immediately wrote a short note of thanks, and tucked it into her handbag to take into work with her, when she returned. She wondered what Damien was doing at that moment, and took a moment to wish him a silent Happy Christmas, before wiping away the tears that were never far from the surface. She sighed, took her presents into her bedroom, and returned to make herself a cup of coffee, before sitting down in front of the television again, hoping to cheer herself up somehow, before turning it off, and going to bed early, for there was nothing to remain awake for. Boxing Day, was going to be worse, she thought to herself, as she prepared for bed - she could go for a walk, but the prospect of being alone for the rest of the day did nothing to cheer her up. The following morning, she ate a small breakfast, washed the dishes, put her coat on, and went out to walk through the silent streets, and out into the countryside, along the riverbank. She was on her way back to the flat, walking past some of the large houses, admiring the decorations that were in the windows, and watching the antics of some children, riding their new bikes and scooters, on the green in front of the houses, when she suddenly saw Steven and his wife Leila emerge from one of the houses. She stopped walking, and watched them, as they walked hand in hand along the road. She wanted to speak to them, but didn't know what to say, so just followed them at a distance, as if she were on her way to the shopping street. They made their way along the High Street, but once there, she lost sight of them, and slowly walked back to her flat. When she got there, she wrote the address down, slipped it into the envelope she had addressed to Jerome, thanking him for her gift, and prepared to cook herself a meal. She admitted to herself she was lonely, but knew that she would be able to meet up with Emma again the next day, and knew she would be pleased to see the other lady again. The afternoon stretched in front of her, and she suddenly remembered Damien's tapes, and decided to listen to them. His voice was so very familiar, similar to Jerome, but not identical, and she wept as she listened to the instructions he was giving at the start of the tape, and remembered the things he had said to her and the way he had spoken, when they had been first married. She got out her laptop, switched it on, and decided to make a start on his notes and tapes. By the time she looked at the clock again, it was nearly 8.00 pm. - she had spent over six hours listening to his voice, typing all his notes, but she had got through another day, and although she had wept copiously, she felt better. Knowing she would have to return the tapes, she made a copy of the first one, so she would have a recording of his voice, that she could listen to whenever she felt the need. She saved her work, switched off the computer, made herself a drink, and prepared for bed.

The following day, she had arranged to meet up with Emma, and made her way to the coffee shop, where she was overjoyed to be reunited with the older lady. They spent a long time, just talking about things – Emma's job, and in particular her boss. "He's gone abroad again, which is why I could spend Christmas away from the house." Emma said "Thinks he's going to be back sometime this week. I hope he is going to be. He's never at home lately. No wonder his wife left him, if he behaved like that when they were together. The poor girl would never have seen

him." she sighed, then, "I shouldn't be telling you this, but he was really depressed a couple of weeks ago. Said his wife had written to him telling him she wanted a divorce, but he can't get in touch with her to talk to her. Says he just wants to have a chat with her, and find out what went wrong. Well, I think I can probably tell you! How the poor girl stood it, him never at home, and his previous housekeeper not allowing her to do anything, I'm not surprised she was fed up. I don't think they were married for very long either."
Alexandra stared at the older woman. "That's not right" she said, "I never..." she stopped herself before she could say something "I mean, it's not right that she was left on her own when he went away. Didn't she have any parents she could visit?"
"Don't know my dear. He doesn't tell me anything about her, just mentions her occasionally, but his sister came to visit one day, when he was at the office, and we got chatting. Very nice woman, I thought. I don't even have an idea of what his wife looks like. He's got a photo of her that he keeps on his desk, but whenever he goes away, he locks the study door, won't let me in there to dust, and if I do go in there, then the photo is put away in a drawer. He doesn't want me to see what she looked like. Probably one of those saucy photos" she grinned at Alexandra, who with a great effort, smiled back. She thought that she knew the photo that Emma was talking about, and although it wasn't too saucy, she wouldn't like anybody else to see it. It had been taken on their honeymoon, she had been in bed, and Damien had taken it of her, as she stretched on

waking. She had been naked, and he had joked he was going to have the photo blown up, which he had done, and kept it in the study at the flat. He had obviously kept it after she had left, but thankfully he was keeping the photo private. Why was he still keeping it, she wondered? She had exchanged gifts with Emma – the older woman had been delighted with the scarf and glove set, and had bought her a writing paper set. It was very pretty and Alexandra was pleased with it. At last, they had said their farewells, arranged to meet again soon, and parted. Alexandra had managed to refrain from giving her address, telling her she was thinking of moving soon, but had given her the number of her mobile phone, and she went back to her flat. She had made herself a cup of tea, and as she drank it, sat thinking about the conversation she had just had with Emma. She had never told the solicitor to tell Damien she wanted a divorce, so she knew she had to go and talk to them again. If they had told him that, she knew she would have to get them to write to him again, telling him that had not been her intention. She made herself a small meal, and then continued transcribing Damien's tapes. By the time she had finished the second tape, it was late, and she was glad to go to bed, for she was due to return to work the following day.

Jerome entered his office after the holiday, and sat down at his desk. It had not been a brilliant Christmas, and he was glad to be back at work. Damien had not been able to return to the United Kingdom in time to spend time with Pandora and himself, Maria's husband had returned a couple of days before the holiday time, and Maria had been delighted to be able to go to their home and spend the Christmas period with him, they had not had any luck in finding Steven's whereabouts, and Alison had not availed herself of their offer of hospitality and they had heard nothing from her. Pandora's mother had spent Christmas with her sister who lived in the North of the country, and they had been unable to celebrate together, so he had spent all his time with Pandora, which he had enjoyed, but as they usually had a houseful of guests, this year had been extremely quiet. Alison had not been in her office when he walked past it, and he wondered how she had spent her holiday. He looked up as he heard voices outside and saw Alison walking towards her office. She came to a halt at the door, wishing him good morning, before she asked him if he'd had a good Christmas, thanked him for his gift, and as he looked at her, his gaze was drawn to the brooch on her coat. "Nice brooch" he said, and she looked at it and smiled. "It was a Christmas present from my landlady. It is pretty, isn't it? She said she'd always liked it, and hoped I would too." she went to the door. "I'll collect your post as soon as it's been delivered, and you can go through it. In the meantime, I'll get on with some of your tapes." and she went to her office. Left alone, Jerome stared after her. The brooch was very familiar. His parents had given it to Nanny Trotter when she had left to have her baby – they had known her name was Anne, and got the brooch to match her initial. It was made of sapphires and diamonds, and they had allowed the boys to wrap it, ready to give to Nanny, when she left the family. That meant that Alison's landlady was Nanny Trotter! He knew he would be able to go and see her again, for they had lost contact after she left, but the family still talked about her, and would have liked to see her again. He would ask Alison when she returned with his post.

An hour later, she was back with the post, and he was on the phone, so he wasn't able to talk to her. However, when he opened the letters, he found among them, an envelope in her hand writing, containing a stiff little note from her, thanking him for her Christmas present. He was on the verge of throwing the envelope into the bin, when he found another piece of paper inside with an address written on it. The note said, “Try this address”, and from the look of it, was near the river in Teddington. When he had finished reading his post, he stood and went into her office. She was typing furiously, but stopped when he entered. “So, what's this?” he asked “and why have I got to try it?”
“I think it’s where your brother might be living” she answered coolly, and was amazed at the glimmer that came into his eyes. “And how did you get this information?” he asked.
“I was out for a walk, when I saw him and his wife leaving the house. If they don't live there, then the people who do, might know their address. It’s just a suggestion” she looked back at her computer screen,
“Why were you out for a walk?” he asked, suspiciously. “I thought you were visiting friends over Christmas?”

"I was, but I came back early, and went for a walk instead." she lied to him, staring at her screen. "Okay" he replied, "I'll accept that. Now, what's the name of your landlady?"
"Why do you want to know that?"
"That's for me to know and you to wonder about." he answered, grinning at her "I promise I'll tell you, if I get some good information."
"Her name is Mrs. Megson. She's a widow with a daughter. She's very good to me."
"I can imagine she would be" he said. "I'll be on the wards if you need me" and he went out of the room. She stared after him, and decided to tell her landlady about his questions, when the old lady came back from staying with her daughter.

That evening, she fed the old lady's cat, for the old lady had returned from her friend's house, and gone away again, reminding Alison to care for the animal, before making herself a small meal, and was sitting in her flat, when the bell went. She glanced out of the window, and saw Jerome standing on her doorstep. She swiftly went downstairs, opened the door, and admitted him. "Sorry, she's not in," she announced, and grinned at his disappointed expression. "Nor is anybody at the address you gave me." he shook his head, "I'm not having a lot of luck locating people at the moment. What with my failure to find the woman that Damien wants to contact, and now nobody else is around. Do you know when Mrs. Megson will be back?"
"Not for a couple of days" she said. "She is staying with her daughter, but I don't know where she lives,

so I'm keeping an eye on the house and feeding the cat for her. She and her daughter had been estranged for a while, and I persuaded Mrs. M. to contact her, and talk to her. She doesn't know, or can't remember what caused the estrangement, so I'm hoping they can talk and make it up. Why don't I let you know when she comes back, and you can come and visit her?" He nodded; "Good idea" he said for it was obvious he wanted to talk to the old lady soon. "Do you want a cup of coffee?" she asked now, and was surprised when he nodded. "I'd love one. Pandora went to see her mother because she couldn't be with us over Christmas, and will be away for a couple of days, so I'm on my own tonight." She led the way upstairs to her flat, and he sat down on the sofa, while she boiled the kettle. "How long have you lived here?" he asked as he looked around him. "Almost 10 months now. I found it, when I needed somewhere to live urgently, and I've been happy here. She's a very good landlady and we're more like friends."

"Where did you live before this then, and where were you working? I know you only started at the hospital a few months ago, but I wondered where you worked before."

"I lived in Richmond in an enormous flat, but I didn't work. I was living with somebody who didn't want me to do anything, or even go anywhere, but when we separated, I knew I had to earn a living, so I applied to the hospital, and got the job as Mr. Williams secretary." she clenched her teeth together, not wanting to say anything more, and Jerome looked at her. "Sorry to hear that" he said

now. "I take it there's no chance of you getting back together with him?" She shook her head. "I don't think so, especially now" as she thought back to her visit to the solicitors, as she placed his coffee in front of him, together with a plate of biscuits. "I'm sorry, but I'm not talking about him anymore. It hurts too much. Please don't ask anything else."
"Okay" he said, knowing she wouldn't say more. She walked across to the kitchen, and picked up her coffee cup, only to put it down again, as her phone rang. It was on the table in front of him, and as it rang, the screen lit up, and he saw a picture of a man, but couldn't see him clearly, and realised this must be the man she had been living with. She answered the phone, with a series of yes and no answers, and arranged a date with somebody, before she said goodbye, and put the phone down on the table again. They talked desultorily about work, before Jerome finished his coffee. "I'll be off" he said. "See you tomorrow" and stood up to go. "Goodnight" she said, as she opened the front door of the flat, and accompanied him as he went through the front door, locked it after him, and went back upstairs. Jerome went to his car, and looked up at the light in the window. It explained a lot about her, he thought, and wondered who the man she had been living with, had been. He must have been really stupid to let her go, he thought, and wondered what, if anything, he could do, to make her happier, as he got into the car and drove away.

Alexandra sat back in her chair, as she heard Jerome's car drive away, and wondered what he would have said if he had seen the photo, she had hanging on her wall in her bedroom. She and Damien had been walking on the Isle of Vatersay, in the Outer Hebrides, and for a while, they had been the only people on the beach. She had taken lots of photos of the surrounding scenery, for she thought it was beautiful, before taking some photos of Damien, and he had caught her to him, taken her in his arms and kissed her, telling her she was more beautiful than the scenery. A woman walking a dog had come onto the beach, and he had asked her to take a photo of them together as they were on their honeymoon, and it showed the pair of them together, their arms around each other. Originally, he had asked the woman to take just one picture of them as they stood together, but then he had pulled her into his arms, and kissed her soundly, and the woman had taken quite a few photos of them, by accident, for she had kept her finger on the button. The photo she had chosen to have enlarged, showed them kissing – it was a great photo, and the best one she had of them together, for she had left all the wedding photos in Damien's flat, and had it made into a picture in a frame. Every night, she looked at it, and wished that time could stand still, and she could go back to how she had felt while the photo was being taken. She knew she would never get rid of it, or any of the photos on her phone. She had printed some of them off, had them made into an album, kept them in her bedside drawer, and every now and then, she would look at them, and remember the good times.

Mrs. Megson returned from staying with her daughter two days later, her face alight with joy. "I've had a great time" she told Alexandra. "My daughter and I had a good time together, and we've made up all our differences. Neither of us can remember exactly why we had a difference of opinion, which made us become estranged, so we're going to be friends again. She went travelling while we were apart, and met her husband abroad. They got married while they were away, she's been married for a couple of years now, and although she hasn't made me a grandmother yet, there's time yet. Her husband has been away, but she's going to bring him here and introduce us very soon. Apparently, they were able to spend Christmas together, but his job entails him travelling to other parts of the country on occasions, but he had to go away the day I went to visit, so I never met him."

"What does he do?" Alexandra asked, unwilling to stop the old lady talking of her happy time. "He's a lawyer" she answered. "Apparently he's a very good one, and does a lot of work for the Foreign Office, which is why they were living abroad for a long time." she smiled at Alexandra. "My daughter took me out every night I was with her, to the theatre or for dinner. They've got a lovely house – it looks out over the river, and it's quite large." Alexandra listened to her landlady's happy talk, and waited for her to ask questions about Alexandra's Christmas. "So, did you have a good time with your friends?" she asked, and Alexandra answered truthfully. "I didn't go anywhere" she said. "I know, I said I was going away, but I didn't do anything. I had a peaceful time, just cooked a meal for myself, went to church, went for a walk, and generally relaxed. But I love your present. Thank you so much. Even my boss commented on it, said it looked very good on my coat. It's much too nice to keep in a drawer, so I'm wearing it on my coat, and it suits it very well." The old lady smirked, as she replied "I'm glad you like it my dear. Hopefully, it will help you. What else did you do?"

"I went to see a lady I helped when she fell over and I gave her a hand. She wanted to keep in touch, and it was nice to see her again. I haven't been able to go before, because she lives with Damien. Turns out she's his new housekeeper, so you can understand why I haven't felt able to go before."

"Oh yes, dear, I can understand that. Does she have your phone number, so she can contact you again?"

"Yes, she phoned a couple of days ago, and I'm going to meet up with her again soon. But I wanted to tell you, that my boss asked me for the name of my landlady, and he wants to meet you." The old lady grinned at her, and Alexandra knew that she was up to something. "What have you done now?" she asked, but Mrs. Megson just smiled. "You'll soon find out dear. I'll tell you very soon." and nothing she could say would alter the old lady's mind.

Alexandra was kept busy over the next couple of days, working for Jerome, for after the holiday, he was busier than ever, so she had lots of work to do for him, typing letters to patients, their general practitioners, and all the paperwork that a consultant surgeon generated. The New Year celebrations came, but Alexandra ignored them, and was in bed and asleep, when midnight struck. She had told Jerome that Mrs. Megson had returned, but he hadn't been to the house again. She was going to go on holiday on Friday evening, and it was on that day, that Jerome bought her a small box, which she recognised as originally belonging to her. Damien had bought it for her when they were first married, and she had kept some small items in it, but now it contained multiple audio tapes. "Don't fret if you can't get them all done," Jerome said, "have a break every day from doing these. Damien doesn't want you to kill yourself with overwork, but he's dictated all these, so thought you would be able to get on with them." Alexandra nodded. "I don't see why I shouldn't get them done" she said now. "I managed to get the first two done in two days, so there's only a few days' work here. I'll get them printed off, and save them for him. I take it he doesn't mind me doing them in the same format as I've used for your book?"

"Not in the least, but Alison, when did you manage to type the tapes? You've not had any free time since I gave them to you, only Christmas and New Year. You didn't do them over Christmas, I hope?" she dropped her eyes to the box, and nodded. "I didn't go anywhere over Christmas," she confessed, "so I wanted to keep busy, and transcribing the audio tapes did that quite nicely."

"So why didn't you come and see us then?" he asked, but she shook her head. "I'm sorry Mr. Ellis, I can't explain. Please don't hold it against me."

"I won't Alison, but remember that if you ever need

anybody to talk to, then I'm here."
"Thank you" she muttered, knowing that she would never take him up on that offer. He was too close to Damien, and as it was him who had caused all her problems, she was not going to talk to his brother.

As she went home that evening, Damien's box in a plastic bag in her hand, she viewed the prospect of two weeks on her own with dismay. At least she would have something to do, to keep her busy, she thought, as she opened the door of the flat. She had cooked herself a small meal, even though she didn't want to eat very much these days, but she was fed up with people telling her that she didn't look very good, that she'd lost too much weight, and urging her to have big meals. She heard the front door bell echo through the hallway downstairs, and knowing that Mrs. Megson wasn't as quick on her feet, she started down the stairs to open the front door. Jerome stood on the doorstep, and smiled at her. "Is she in?" he asked, and she nodded. "I'll just go and knock on her door for you." she offered, and allowed him to enter the house. She knocked on Mrs. Megson's front door, and when the old lady called her to come in, opened it, said "You've got a visitor Mrs. Megson", and stood back to allow Jerome to enter. "Nanny Trotter" he exclaimed. "More beautiful than ever" he declared, taking the older lady in his arms, and embracing her. "Mr. Jerome" said Mrs. Megson. "Oh, my goodness, you do look well." Alexandra watched the reunion, but knew she couldn't stay, and silently slipped away, shut the door and went back up to her flat, leaving the old lady with her erstwhile charge.

“However, did you know which one I was?” Jerome asked, the old lady, as they sat drinking the tea she had made and his old Nanny smiled. “It's easy telling you apart from the others.” she said now. “The difference between Mr. Damien and Mr. Steven isn't as easy, but I can see it. Remember, I bought you up until you were seven years old. I haven't seen any of you for so long, but its lovely to see you again, Mr. Jerome.” They sat for a long time, just talking, catching up on the past, before Jerome declared he would have to go, but they would catch up again. “Why don't you come to my house tomorrow?” he asked, “I'm not on call, so you could meet Pandora, my wife, and we can have a meal, and talk about the past, and catch up on what we've been doing.”

“You're up to something Mr. Jerome. I always knew when you were plotting something.”

“You know me too well, Nanny” Jerome laughed, “but yes, I do want to try and do something, but I'll let you know if I can manage it tomorrow.” They made arrangements for the following day, and Jerome left the house with a lighter heart.

Chapter Seven

The following morning, Jerome made his way to the address he had been given by Alexandra, and taking a deep breath, he rang the doorbell. The door was answered by a very elegant woman, who looked at him with shock. “You've got to be one of Steven's brothers” she declared. “It's like looking in a mirror.” Jerome nodded. “I'm Jerome” he said, “Is Steven in?” The woman nodded. “Come in.” she smiled. “He's in the kitchen. I'm Leila, his wife.” she introduced herself, as she opened the door wide for him. “Steven,” she called, as she shut the door behind him, “Steven, you've got a visitor.” She put her finger to her lips, urging Jerome to be quiet, as he could hear footsteps coming towards the front room door. The door was opened, and Jerome saw his estranged brother, framed in the doorway. “Bloody hell! Jerome!” Steven exclaimed, throwing his arms around his brother, and embracing him. “Oh my God, I can't believe it. How the hell did you find me? I've been trying to locate you for ages with no success.”

“I had help” Jerome said, as the two men hugged.

“Take your brother inside” Leila urged, and Jerome was led into a large light room, with a fire burning merrily in the fireplace. “I'll make coffee” she declared, as she went out into the kitchen, leaving the two men together. There was an outburst of talk, as they started speaking catching up on the past, before Leila returned with the coffee tray. “Sorry, darling,” Steven spoke, as he stood to take the tray from her. "I haven't introduced you. This is my brother Jerome. Jerome, my wife Leila." Jerome smiled. "We introduced ourselves on the doorstep" he said, and Leila handed round the coffee cups. "So, what's happened to Damien? Do you still see him?" Steven asked, mentioning the third member of the trio for the first time. "Oh, he's around. He doesn't live too far away, in Richmond, and I live here in Teddington, about five miles away from him. But he's been abroad lately, so I don't know whether or not he's back. I'll phone him in a bit, and if he's back, then perhaps we could all have a meal tonight. I've got another friend of mine coming to have a meal, and I know she'd like to meet up with everybody." Leila looked at her husband, "I was going to take Steven to Mum's house tonight, but we could do that tomorrow. I haven't made any special plans, so it could be interesting to meet up with other members of your family."

Jerome looked from one to the other, "Please do come, we can sit and talk and catch up on the past, and you can meet my wife, Pandora." Steven and Leila nodded, and the talk became general again. "So how did you find out where I was living?" Steven asked, and Jerome grinned at his brother's question.

"My secretary" he said. "She knew that Damien and I were identical twins, but didn't know there was a third member of the family, and she mentioned that she'd seen somebody identical to me walking down Teddington High Street, but she thought it was a doppelganger, because as she said, she knows everybody has one somewhere. She had no idea you and I were related at that time. I explained, told her why I was looking, and left it at that. She said she'd seen you come out of this house over the Christmas period, and made a note of the address, and gave it to me. I did come to visit a few days ago, but there was nobody in."

"It was probably when I took Mum out for dinner, but Steven wasn't even here then. He'd had to go up country, and he only got back last night." Leila answered her brother-in-law.

"So, what do you do now, to have a job that requires you to work over the Christmas period?" Jerome asked and added, "It's different for me, because medical staff know what they're letting themselves in for, but other professions don't normally work over the holiday."

"So, you did manage to qualify." Steven said "When we were at Uni, you were the one who wanted to be a doctor, and you were doing your medical degree, and I thought you'd have managed it, but I didn't know if you'd succeeded. As for me, I'm a lawyer. That law degree came in handy after all."

"But you didn't finish your degree!" Jerome exclaimed, "When you left Uni, we were in our third year, we were about to break up for the Spring holidays, and one day you were there, we'd all been to a party with friends the previous evening, we were getting ready to go home the following day, but when I went to your room the next day, you'd gone. What on earth happened to make you leave so suddenly?"

Steven stared at him in disbelief. "You were told what I'd done" he said now, "They promised to let you know where I was, and what I was doing."

"They?" queried Jerome, wondering what he'd missed. Steven looked astounded at his brothers' questions. "I was head hunted" he said quietly. "My tutors asked if I would do some undercover work for the," he broke off, then started speaking again, "I was told I had to leave Uni very quickly and quietly, but my parents and siblings would be told where I was, and given an idea of what I was doing. I spent a few years doing something which I can't talk about even now, and when that was finished, I completed my law degree, but at a different University. Do you mean it, nobody told you what I was doing?"
"Nobody told us a thing. We thought we'd done something to upset you, and you'd just left Uni, and didn't want any more contact with us. I'm sorry to have to tell you, that Pa died about four years ago, never knowing what had happened to you, and Mother still has no idea. She aged about 10 years when you disappeared, and when Pa became so ill, I don't think he wanted to carry on living. She's living in the Algarve at the moment with the two youngsters. They've both got jobs out there, and I don't think they'll be back in the country very soon. Mother and Pa moved after you'd gone, they said they couldn't stay in a house that reminded them so much of you, so you wouldn't have had their new address, and the two youngsters went with them. We don't have much to do with them nowadays. We speak on the phone of course, and I've visited them, but we don't see each other that often. I don't think they've even been in the country for the last few years." He stopped suddenly, "No, tell a lie, they did come over about a year ago. They'd arranged a big

get together to meet Damien's wife, and then he had to go to Brussels at the last minute, so it didn't happen. They all flew back the following day."
"Damien's married as well?" Steven said, and grinned. "She must be somebody special, to have caught Damien, knowing how he only ever wanted the best things or people. What's she like?"
"I have no idea. They got married while I was abroad, so I've never met her, and he doesn't have any photos of her on show. I've seen one photo of her, and all that registered is that she has blonde hair and blue eyes." he sighed, "She left him and completely disappeared, less than a year ago, and I only got back into the country about six months ago. Since then, I've been trying to help him find her, but it's been difficult. Damien's changed a lot since she went."
"Poor Damien, and poor Ma. I must phone her, and let her know I'm okay, tell her what happened, and I do want to maintain contact with her. It explains why I haven't been able to contact her, if she's living in the Algarve now." Steven was sympathetic. "And if you were out of the country, that explains why you weren't on any electoral registers. But why did Damien's wife go?"
"Various reasons, and I'll let him tell you about that, if he wants to. As I said, he's changed now, not so light hearted, and is very rarely in the country now, as he's busy working. He's a very busy man, disappearing off round the world, to help different governments manage their money. I wonder if he hasn't taken on so much work, to try and forget his wife. He's said he's going to give that up if Alexandra ever comes back, but I very much doubt that." The

two men continued talking, and Leila, knowing they were going to continue talking and catching up on the past for a while yet, left the room, to phone her mother, and see how she was. She knew she had been very remiss in not keeping in contact with her mother, and wanted to make amends, but the old lady was proud, and wouldn't accept any help from her daughter.

At length, Jerome left, after making arrangements for their visit to his house that evening, and got home. He told Pandora what he had done, and his wife, who had a very good sense of humour, was amused by the arrangements he had made. Lastly, he phoned Damien, relieved to find out that he was back in the country, told him to be at the house that evening, and refused to tell him why he needed to be there. That evening, when Damien arrived, he greeted him, wanting to know what he had been up to, and telling him what he had given Alison as a gift. He took his brother into the front room, and when the front door bell rang, to announce Steven's arrival, had arranged for Pandora to answer. From the silence, when she opened the door, she was as surprised, as Leila had been, when she opened the door to Steven and his wife, and he looked forward to seeing the expression on his brothers faces, when they came face to face with each other, after such a long time. The door opened, and he watched Damien's face, as he beheld the visitor. There was a moment's silence, then the two men embraced and started talking nineteen to the dozen. There was great hilarity, as the three of them caught up with what had happened in the intervening years, and the two wives became better acquainted. They were talking nonstop, as the doorbell rang again, and Jerome went to the front door, to admit Nanny Trotter. "I've got a surprise for you" he murmured to her, and flung the door open. Even he was surprised, when Leila cried, "Mother" and ran to meet her, as at the same time, Steven and Damien, cried "Nanny". There was a great up rush of emotion as the three men became re-acquainted with their old Nanny, who proved to be Leila's mother. At length, Pandora insisted that they all sit down to a very late dinner, and the meal that followed, was eaten in an atmosphere of hilarity and fun. It was as they were sitting over coffee afterwards, that Nanny spoke. "It's a pity you're not married, Mr. Damien. It would be good if you were able to settle down and become a happily married man."

"I am married Nanny. She left me." he refused to enlarge on that statement, but turned to his brother. "Actually Steven, regarding that, I do need to ask you a question. When did you get back to this country? And would you and Leila have been in London last year, on the 16th of February?" Steven looked at Leila, and they nodded and smiled, before he answered.

"Yes, we were in London then. That was the day I got back into the country. Leila had come back here before me, to look for a house, but she couldn't get to the airport, and we arranged to meet up again at a certain point in town, and she came to collect me. We were staying in a hotel near Richmond Park for a few weeks, before we found our house, and we finally moved in about eight months ago. Why are you asking?"

"Because when my wife walked out, she left me a note saying that she'd seen me kissing a woman on more than one occasion, when I knew that I'd not been out of the office all day, and when Jerome and I were talking about it, we wondered whether she could have seen you and Leila. You and I are so identical, she could have confused us I suppose. Where did you and Leila meet up?" he asked, and when Steven replied, "One of the side streets near John Lewis in Oxford Street." he nodded. "That's got to be the explanation. I know Xandra often went shopping near there. I haven't been able to find her to ask her where she had seen me, with another woman."

"Didn't you ever tell her that you had brothers who looked like you?" asked Mrs. Megson, and Damien shook his head. "I wanted to surprise her" he muttered, "so I didn't tell her anything. I'd told her I had brothers, but not that we were identical."

"Idiot boy" she said, and Damien nodded. "Don't I know it" he said. "I'm the one who's reaping the rewards of my idiocy now." he stood, said "Excuse me" and walked out of the room. There was a silence after he had left, until Jerome spoke softly. "Leave him for a while" he said, "he's got a lot on his mind lately, but he'll be okay in a while. He'll be back in a bit, in a better mood than he is at the moment, but we've got to do something for him. If Alexandra did see you and Leila, Steven, then that will explain a lot." The party continued, and after a while, Damien returned to the room, and tried to join in the talk, but he didn't stay long. "I'm going to make a move" he said softly to Jerome. "I need to think about things, if you don't mind. I'm sorry to break up the party, but now we know where we all live, we can keep in touch. I'll be in touch soon." and after bidding everybody good night, he left the house to go home to think about things.

Alexandra had decided that she needed a complete break, and spent one week of her two weeks annual leave away from the flat. She had wanted to return to the Outer Hebrides, to try and relive the happy times she had had there with Damien, but she knew it was an impractical idea, for she could not drive and a car was almost a necessity on the islands, so resigned herself to finding somewhere else to go. Instead, she had gone to stay at a hotel in Oxford, visiting the city's museums and colleges, for the city held no memories for her, and she knew she wouldn't have to contend with those. There were no crowds, for the new term hadn't started again, and although she was alone again, she was in different surroundings. At the end of the week, she returned to the flat, and continued with typing Damien's manuscript. She had phoned Emma, keeping her fingers crossed that Damien would not answer the phone, and arranged to meet her again, away from Damien's house, and they had gone out to the theatre one evening. She went to the gym she belonged to, and enjoyed swimming in the pool, but soon left, unwilling to stay alone, amid the happy laughing crowds. When Sunday evening came around, she was glad, for she was looking forward to going back to work the following day, and meeting up with her colleagues again, for she had been very lonely while she wasn't working, but she thought to herself, that was normal. All Damien's typing was done, and she returned the tapes to the box, and along with the manuscript she had produced, she put them into a bag, to take back into the hospital on the following day.

She had been back at work for two days, when she was asked to go and give message to a member of staff, so left her office, and went out into the main body of the hospital, and made her way to her destination, and pass the message on. She was on her way back, when she was stopped by a nurse going in the opposite direction. "Alexandra Taylor-Ellis as I live and breathe." declared a well-remembered voice, and Alexandra looked up to see the happy smiling face of Beatrice Spence, her closest friend from her training days, and one of the witnesses to her marriage to Damien. "Bea" she cried, and the two girls embraced. "Oh, it's lovely to see you again" Alexandra said, as she looked closely at her friend, but Bea didn't return the sentiment. "What the hell are you doing here? And what on earth have you done to your hair? I almost didn't recognise you." asked Bea, and Alexandra knew that Bea would want to know everything that had happened. "Why on earth didn't you answer any of my phone calls, and how's your gorgeous husband?" she continued, and Alexandra looked puzzled. "What phone calls?" Alexandra seized on the first question, "If you phoned, I never got any messages. I tried to contact you so many times, but I could never get hold of you at the nurses' home, so I gave up eventually."

"I phoned you practically every day after you came back from your honeymoon, for at least three or four weeks. I didn't have your new mobile number, after you'd lost your phone before you got married, so I had to phone the land line. I was assured by your housekeeper that you were receiving my messages, but you never got back to me. I wrote a couple of times as well, and sent you a card on your birthday, but you never replied. I carried on phoning and visiting the flat for at least a couple of months, but you were never in, and I was worried about you, but I reckoned you were away with Damien, travelling with him, but then life got busier, and I'm afraid I gave up I was going to tell you I'd got a new job here in this hospital. I'm the senior staff nurse on women's medical."

"Congratulations" Alexandra said, then, "Hang on, you said you visited as well?" she frowned, then thought for a second and asked, "When are you off duty?" and Bea replied, "Now. Why?"

"Are you doing anything this afternoon?" she asked, "Would you come home with me and we can have a talk, and I'll tell you everything? I haven't been able to talk to anybody for a long time, and you can explain what you meant about visiting."

"Of course I can. Let me go and get changed, and I'll wait for you by the front entrance. We've got so much to catch up on."

"I've just got to go and let my boss know I'm going

home. I'll say I've got a migraine, and hope they believe me."
"What boss, and why aren't you in uniform?" Bea asked, but Alexandra shook her head. "I'll explain everything when we get home" she said, and arranging where and when to meet, the two girls parted. Alexandra hurried upstairs, told Patricia she was going home because she felt unwell, and went out of the hospital, where she met up with Bea at the gates. She swiftly led the other girl to the flat, and let her in. "Why on earth are you living in this poky little flat?" she asked, looking around her, "Did Damien lose all his money? His old flat was lovely."
"It still is. I'm not living with Damien any more" she answered, and burst into tears. Bea took one look at her friend, and gave her a big hug. "No wonder you want to talk" she said, "I'll make you a cuppa, then you can sit down and tell me all about it." and Alexandra had to do as she was told. Bea looked at her friend with astonishment, as she filled the kettle, and found the teabags and mugs. She and Damien had been so happy on their wedding day, and before that, when they had been courting. What on earth had happened to them, that Alexandra was living on her own, in such a different place? The tea had been made, and the two girls sat drinking it, as Alexandra told her friend everything – how the housekeeper had tried to control her, wouldn't let her do anything in the flat, didn't want her to stay in the flat when Damien wasn't there, and now it appeared that she had failed to pass on messages about visits or phone calls, and even destroyed personal letters. "I would have been in when you visited as well" she said, "but

obviously she didn't tell me that you were at the door." Alexandra told her of her feeling of loneliness, without any friends, while Damien was away a lot of the time, and finally how she had seen him with another woman. "Well," Bea's voice was cold, "it sounds as if he changed completely, after you were married. I think you did right, walking out on him then" she declared, but Alexandra stopped her, shaking her head. "I haven't told you the rest. I'm not nursing, because I wanted to do something different and I couldn't face nursing again, especially as I'd met Damien when I was on the wards, so I'm a secretary to one of the consultants. I was Mr. Williams secretary, but he left about two months ago, and my new boss was appointed. I met him, and nearly passed out, because he looks so much like Damien. Apparently, he's, his brother. They're twins, but then I saw another man along the High Street here, and he's absolutely identical to Damien in every way, and it turns out that there are three of them. They're identical triplets! Steven, the third brother, is the guy I saw kissing another woman, and she is his wife. So, I'd walked out on Damien for nothing! He never told me that he was one of three, and they were completely identical! But I can't admit I made a mistake and go back to him. He was never at home anyway, and I didn't find out until a few weeks ago, that he'd sacked the housekeeper because he found out what she'd been doing. I'll bet he never knew about the phone calls, letters or visits though." Bea was silent after Alexandra's explanation, and she took her friend's hand. "I don't know what to say" she said eventually. "Has he served you with divorce

papers yet?"
Alexandra shook her head. "He doesn't know where I live, and I hope he doesn't find out. But I discovered that he was trying to find me, so I asked my solicitors to tell him that if he wanted a divorce, I wouldn't contest it, but his new housekeeper, who I met after I helped her, when she had an accident, told me that his wife had written to him, saying she wanted a divorce, but I've never said that. I need to talk to my solicitors again, and see what they actually said in the letter they sent him, but I haven't been able to get in touch with them. They tell me that they'll call back, but they never do. But Bea, I still love him, I don't want to divorce him, and I'd love us to get back together again. But he'd have to change if I went back to him."
"So why don't you phone him and talk to him again?"
"Would you?" she asked, and Bea thought for a minute then shook her head. "No. I can understand why you're feeling so depressed obviously. Did you lose contact with everybody from the hospital as well as me?"
"Yes," she replied. "Everybody seemed to be so envious of my new lifestyle, but they didn't want to keep in contact, so I never managed to be able to talk to them again. Fair weather friends, all of them." Bea shook her head.
"I don't think they were. I think the housekeeper did to them, what she did to me. Took the phone messages, but didn't pass them on. I know at least five of our friends who said that you never called them, when they'd tried to contact you, so they didn't push it. But why didn't you tell him you were

so fed up?" Alexandra stared at her friend in disbelief.

"You mean they did want to stay friends? Oh, that's just dandy! Not only did she want to control my life, she wanted to stop me having any friends as well. Bea, I did try and tell him that I wasn't happy. Damien didn't listen to me telling him that I was bored with his way of life, he accused me of not wanting to go to receptions with him, and had no interest when I tried to explain why I didn't want to go to them. They were absolutely horrible. Damien and I were always separated at the dinner table, and my dinner partners didn't talk to me. After we'd eaten, the men would go into another room, and I'd be left with the women, who were nearly always elderly and the English ones didn't want to talk to me, they'd got their own little cliques, and I was excluded, or if they were foreigners, none of them spoke very good English, and if I could understand them, the only things they wanted to talk about was their grandchildren or the difficulty of getting decent help in the home. But most of the time, they didn't talk to me at all, and I was always alone. I remember one reception I went to; I said hello to the people who were hosting it, when we arrived, and then didn't say another word until Damien was taking me home! The hosts didn't even say goodbye to me! Of course I got bored, and didn't want to go to the damn things! And then Damien got a lot busier, was never at home, he was always off abroad somewhere, and he wouldn't tell me what he was doing, just said he was busy working. He spent nearly six months of the eleven we were together,

abroad! We had a major row one evening, when I was so fed up with him never being there, I accused him of being too busy to be able to spend any time with me, but he just ignored that, said I obviously didn't want him to do his job, and it was the day following that, that I saw him and this other woman together, but it turns out it wasn't him, after all." Bea looked sympathetically at her friend. "No wonder you've lost weight. You look so thin and what on earth have you done to your hair? It looks awful. You've got lovely blonde hair, so why did you want to change it?"
"I needed to alter my appearance, just in case Damien ever came to Teddington, and by some freak chance, saw me. I don't think he would, but just in case..." she tailed off and Bea nodded. Poor Alex, she thought, she was obviously very lonely, and missing her husband. "We're going to have to keep in contact" Bea said, "I know we're both working at the same hospital, but I had no idea you were there. Look, why don't we swap phone numbers now and we can get together again soon?" They were soon chatting eagerly together, laughing about incidents that had occurred in their training days and when they had been trained, and after she had cooked them both a meal, when at last Bea left, promising to keep in touch, she felt happier than she had done for a long time.

When she returned to work the following day, she felt very guilty as her colleagues asked her if she were fully recovered. Jerome was especially attentive to her, and after a long session of dictation, he motioned her to stay where she was, and thanked her for her assistance in finding his missing brother. "I don't think we'd have managed it, if it hadn't been for you." he said "Our whole family is grateful to you, for all the help you've given us. You'll have to come for a meal with all of us, and we can thank you, and you can meet the rest of the family. But I've got to explain why I wanted to know your landlady's name as well. She was our Nanny, when we were younger, and we always referred to her as Nanny Trotter, which was her maiden name. I recognised your brooch, as one that my parents gave her, when she left to have her daughter. They allowed us boys to wrap it up and give it to her on her last day. Sapphires and diamonds look very good together, don't they? Anyway, as you know, I met up with your landlady, and re-introduced her to the rest of the family, and then found out that her daughter is married to our other brother, Steven, and we're all overjoyed to be back in contact with each other again. So, thanks Alison, we're all very grateful." Somehow, Alexandra got herself out of his office, and into her own, to sit down heavily at the desk. The brooch was Sapphires and Diamonds, she thought, and very valuable! She resolved to make sure that Mrs. Megson got it back as soon as she could arrange it.

That evening, she put the brooch back into its box, and took it downstairs to her landlady and returned it to her. "I can't accept it" she said. "I didn't realise it was so valuable. It's served its purpose, because I know what you wanted to achieve, and you've done that now. You're reconciled with your daughter, who is married to one of Damien's brothers, and you've been reunited with all three of them. Thank you for lending it to me, but I can't keep it." and she had left it in the old ladies' hands, and gone back up to her own rooms. Mrs. Megson watched her go, knowing that she had started something, she hoped would make Alison feel a lot happier.

She had left Damien's manuscript, tapes and the box on Jerome's desk, and apart from thanking her, he had said nothing more about it. However, a couple of days after she had taken the afternoon off, she found an envelope on her desk, containing a cheque for a very large amount, from Damien, together with a short letter of thanks from him. As she read it, she began to cry again, and had to run to the ladies' room, where she stood, crying bitter tears. Damien's handwriting was so familiar to her, and she knew that she wanted to talk to him again, and hear his voice, calling her Xandra as he had always done. Eventually, her tears dried and she knew that she had to be strong. Resolutely, she wiped her eyes, blew her nose, and went back to her desk, where she sat typing furiously. Jerome walked past her office, looked in and saw her distress, but didn't say anything, but he did wonder what or who had upset her again, for she had appeared happier than she had been for a long time, when he had seen her just before he had put the envelope on her desk.

"Wondered if you would be able to do some more

typing for Damien?" Jerome asked her a day before her next annual leave, and she nodded. "Just leave everything on the desk if I'm not in the office" she said. "Was the last lot satisfactory?" and he nodded and smiled at her. "When he looked at it, he said it was obvious you'd worked for an author before, because it was all done so well. He was very impressed. I think that was evident in the cheque he sent."

"I'm glad he thought it was so good." she said. "But he's mistaken about me having worked for an author before. I've never done that."

"So, who did you work for, before you worked for Mr. Williams?" Jerome asked, and she hesitated. She'd never worked for anybody else, as she'd been a nurse before she married. "Oh, I worked for an agency, and got sent all over the place" she prevaricated, and thankfully, he accepted her answer. She was glad when he left her office, and she was able to leave the hospital that evening and be on her own away from Jerome who reminded her so very much of Damien. She phoned Bea, invited her to dinner, and the cinema, and that evening, she enjoyed herself with her friend, and resolved to enjoy her next week of annual leave.

Chapter Eight

Alexandra's second annual leave, was more enjoyable than the first, for this time she knew she had somebody to talk to occasionally. She spent some of the time, typing more of Damien's book, but she also took time away from the computer, to spend time with Bea, when she was off duty, and the two girls decided to go out for a drive in Bea's small car, and drove out into the country. "You can map read, Alex," Bea commanded, so she had done just that. However, she managed to misread the map, and they had ended up totally lost, in a small Essex village, that didn't appear to be on the map, but they had found a tea room, and Bea had insisted that they eat a large cream cake each. "If you lose any more weight, you're going to fade away." she said. "How much do you weigh now?"

"Oh, stop moaning at me" she said, "I don't know how much I weigh, and I am eating again."

"Only when somebody nags you" had been the response, and although she denied it, she knew it was true. She could count every rib, she thought that evening, as she stood under the shower, but maybe that was a good thing. She didn't really want to eat anything, but forced herself to eat a small meal, then, and on the following days she was off duty. She had three days extra off duty and as Bea's steady boyfriend hadn't been able to get any time off, she and Bea had decided to go out together again for the day. As they drove away from the flat, they stopped at a junction to allow a large Bentley to go past, and Alexandra looked after it, for Damien had owned one. She glanced at the driver as the car passed her, and saw that her husband was driving it. She watched it go, but he did not slacken speed, and it soon disappeared from sight. She almost burst into tears again, and Bea pulled over to the side of the road, handed her a box of tissues, and told her to let it all out. "I know who it was, and if the sight of him makes you cry, then perhaps it's just as well that you're not going to be able to live with him again. If you did, you'd spend all day in tears, and make yourself really ill." Alexandra sighed, wiped her eyes, blew her nose, and smiled at her friend. "Oh, Bea, I've really missed you." she said, "you make me smile again. I'm so pleased we managed to meet up again." Bea checked her rear-view mirror, and saw a traffic warden approaching, before driving off again. "If I stay there any longer, I'll get a ticket" she said. "So, where are we going to go today?" They made a decision to go out to the Cotswolds, and Bea drove away. Their visit to the Cotswolds was fun, and they had had an excellent lunch in a pub, which both girls had enjoyed very much, and they were on their way home, and back in their own hospital region, driving down a narrow country lane, behind a larger car, when another car came around a corner, very fast, and the two cars collided. There was a great deal of twisted metal, steam and cries from both drivers. "Hell!" said Bea, braking sharply, and pulling into the side of the road behind the two cars that were entangled. The two girls were out of the car, and giving assistance, for it was obvious that the two drivers were badly injured. Alexandra had phoned for help, before she went to assist Bea, and help the drivers. The two men had suffered quite severe injuries, and both girls were kept busy. When an ambulance arrived along with the police, both drivers were assessed and loaded into the ambulance to be taken to hospital. The senior paramedic looked at the first aid given by the two girls, and congratulated them on knowing what to do. "Well, if we didn't know, as trained nurses, we'd be shot" Bea announced, and Alexandra agreed with her friend's statement. "Shall I go with them?" Alexandra asked and as Bea nodded, she got into the back of the ambulance, to help the paramedic keep an eye on the patients, and was driven away. When the ambulance arrived at the hospital, she handed over her patient to the sister in charge, and gave her a report of what had happened, and what they had done. She walked away, watched, if she had but known it, by Jerome, who had been called down to the A&E Department, to assist. When she had left the department, he had seen to the patients, and after they had been taken to the ward, Jerome asked one of the staff nurses who had looked after the patients, what their initial treatment had been like. "It was great" she said, "whoever looked after them, knew exactly what they were doing. The patient I was looking after had his life saved by the person who was looking after him. He would have bled to death without help" and she gave details. Jerome nodded, as the staff nurse continued "The only way they could have been treated better, was if there had been a doctor on the scene. Apparently, the paramedics were very impressed with their treatment"

"So, could one nurse and a non-medical person have done such a good job?"
"No," was the answer. "There were obviously two nurses on the job. They both needed expert care, and they both got it."
"Thanks Staff" he said, before he made his way to the ward, but his thoughts were disturbed, and he made a mental note to talk to Alison when she came back to work.

Two days later, Alexandra was back at work after her leave. She had woken that morning, with a bit of a sore throat, and didn't feel brilliantly well, so when she walked into Jerome's office to take dictation, she was unprepared for his questions at the end of the session. "Did you enjoy your time off?" he asked and at her nod, he asked where she had been. "Oh, I met up with a friend of mine, and we went out for a couple of days. She works here as well, and we enjoyed ourselves. We went for a day out in Essex, and then had a day in the Cotswolds. Made pigs of ourselves eating giant cream cakes, and enormous meals." She smiled at the memory. "Anything happen while you were away?" he asked, and her smile faded, as she shot him a sideways glance
"What kind of thing?" she asked
"Oh, like car crashes, something like that?"
"Well, we did see a crash, but we weren't involved in it."
"Alison, stop lying to me please. I've talked to one of the nurses in A&E, and she tells me that the treatment given to the men, was so good, that you had to be trained. You are a trained nurse, aren't

you?"

"Why do you think that?"

"I was called down to A&E after the patients you bought in, needed some assistance. They're both doing very well, by the way, but the nurses said that they had to have been looked after by two trained nurses, and the paramedics were full of how good the first responders had been. So, please tell me the truth. You are trained, aren't you?" She nodded, almost relieved to admit it. "So why don't you work as a nurse now? Not that you're not a good secretary, because you are, but I just wondered why you don't nurse? There's a severe shortage of nurses in this hospital, as you must be aware."

"I told you that I'd been living with somebody, and I'd left him? Well, I met him when I was nursing, and I didn't feel that I could stand to nurse again, because it would have too many memories which I didn't want to bring to the surface again. I'd just started to be able to forget them, and now, what with everything that's happened, the memories are resurfacing again"

"What was his name?" he asked gently, but she shook her head. "That's my secret Mr. Ellis, and I'm not telling anybody."

"Okay," he said, "I won't ask any more, but now you're back, we'll have to make a date when you come to dinner" she nodded, although she had no intention of going to dinner with him and his family. She stood then, and went back to her own office to work.

That evening, Mrs. Megson had been out again

with her daughter, and Alexandra had the odd feeling that the old lady would soon be going to live with her daughter permanently. She had walked past Steven's house again, and seen that the house actually had a granny annexe, and she wondered if the plan was for Mrs. Megson to sell her house, and go to live with her daughter. Steven and Leila were frequent visitors, or one or other would come to the house to collect the old lady and take her with them. She had avoided having much contact with Steven as much as she could, because he was so similar facially, to Damien, and she didn't think she'd be able to retain control, if she had too much to do with him. She was tired, so had showered and changed ready for bed, before making herself a hot drink, and took some more Paracetamol, because her throat wasn't getting better. She had been feeling off colour for a couple of days now, and she was a bit hoarse as well, her voice was slightly altered, and was almost grateful for that, when the doorbell of the house rang. Mrs. Megson was out with her daughter, so she had to answer the door. She went downstairs, and looked through the spy hole, and recoiled, for there standing on the doormat, was Damien. "Hello" she called. "Can I help you?"
"I just wanted to come and thank you for helping me out. I understand that you've done all my typing, and you did a brilliant job."
"Oh, thank you." she answered him. "I enjoyed doing it. I'm sorry I can't invite you in, because I'm in my night dress" she said, and was relieved when he answered,
"Okay, that's alright. I'll leave the cheque I've got for

you with Jerome. I might ask you to do some more at some time in the future, if you're amenable."
"Yes, I don't mind doing more typing." she replied.
"I have no doubt we'll meet when Jerome invites you to dinner." he said, "I'm looking forward to that. Thanks very much and goodnight." and she watched through the spyhole as he made his way away from the front door. She leaned against the door, wiping away the tears that spilled from her eyes. She made up her mind to talk to the solicitors again. She had not heard anything from them, despite phoning on several occasions, and asking them to contact her, and she wanted to know exactly what they had said to Damien, to give him the wrong impression about her intentions, and she didn't think they were very good at their job. She took herself off to bed then, to stare at the photo on the wall, and to lie and think about Damien. The following morning, when she awoke, her throat was even worse than it had been. It hurt to swallow properly, and she knew she was in for a bad cold, and was going to need more Paracetamol and some throat lozenges to soothe her sore throat. She bought them on the way to work, and got through the day by eating a packet of them. Jerome had been out of the office all day, but left a pile of work on her desk, and she hadn't seen him to talk to. She had started to cough as well, which hurt her chest. On the way home that evening, she bought a couple more packets of throat sweets, knew that she shouldn't be eating as many as she was, bought some more Paracetamol as well, and went home to bed, not bothering to eat anything. Luckily, it was the weekend now, and she knew she'd

have two days to get better, before she had to go back to work.

On Saturday, she managed to get through the day somehow. She didn't want to get up, or eat anything, so spent the day in bed, just dozing or getting up to make herself a drink or two, but she wasn't hungry, so didn't eat anything. Mrs. Megson was out all of the day, spending time with Leila and Steven, so there was nobody in the house. She went to sleep that night, hoping that the pain killers she had taken, would soon take effect.

By the time Sunday came around, she knew she wasn't at all well – the Paracetamol hadn't helped at all, her throat felt as if she'd swallowed barbed wire, and her cough was worse than it had ever been, and she hadn't had much sleep, because the cough was keeping her awake. She was hot and sweating, but felt cold. She felt as if she were in a dream world, and although she could hear her phone ringing, and knew she should answer it, she couldn't be bothered to get up to find it, and do so. She dozed off again, as the phone stopped ringing, and lay back against the pillows, trying to find a comfortable position to sleep, for she coughed ceaselessly when she lay down to sleep.

She was woken by the sound of the doorbell, but couldn't get out of bed to answer it, and when the bedroom door was opened and Bea walked in, she accepted it as part of the dream she was having. "Oh God, Alex, what on earth's the matter with you?" she said. Alexandra could see another figure in the doorway, and knew it was her landlady, but just accepted it. She coughed painfully again, and closed her eyes, and slipped back into a disturbed sleep.

Bea felt her friends' pulse – it was racing, felt her forehead, and it was obvious that Alex had a very high temperature. She looked around her, and wondered how long Alex had been ill. Mrs. Megson came into the room, and looked down at Alex. "I think she needs some antibiotics," Bea said to her now, and the old lady nodded. "I've been out and I haven't seen her for a couple of days, so I didn't know she was so unwell, otherwise I'd have done something. Do you want me to call Mr. Jerome? He's a doctor, and I don't know if Alison is registered with a local GP." Bea shook her head, "She wouldn't get to see anybody very easily anyway, because it's a weekend. But she needs some help and soon. She's sweating profusely, she's got a high temperature, and her pulse is really rapid. Her cough isn't helping her, and she needs a decent night's sleep. I think she's got pneumonia. I could call for an ambulance, but if her boss is a doctor, he might be better."
"I'm going to call Mr. Jerome" Mrs. Megson said decisively. "If she needs to go to hospital, then he'll be able to arrange it." and she went out of the room, and Bea could hear her going downstairs. Bea stayed with her friend, and went to look in the fridge. "I don't think she's eaten anything for a long time, and the milk has gone off, so she hasn't had much to drink for a while. I've got to try and get her to drink something" she muttered to herself, and found a

glass, which she filled with water, and took to Alexandra. The other girl was thrashing around in the bed, not sleeping naturally, coughing every time she moved, and Bea knew she had no chance of getting any fluid into the girl. Mrs. Megson came back upstairs, "I've been in touch with Mr. Jerome, he's coming to see if he can help. Is there anything I can do to help her?"
"Don't think so Mrs. M. Thanks for letting me in. She needs medical help, and I hope she'll get it. When I rang and got no answer, I knew there was something wrong. She always answers her phone, no matter what happens." She glanced round the room, seeing the photo of Alex and Damien, thought about taking it down in case Jerome saw it, but decided not to do so. Damien wanted to talk to her, and find her, she thought, so if a member of his family saw the photo, it might help her friend.

Jerome arrived swiftly, and when Mrs Megson opened the door to him, he went upstairs, to stop aghast at the sight of Alexandra. She was pale, but sweating, coughing badly, and when he put his hand on her forehead, he could feel that she had a very high temperature Bea looked at him and smiled as she recognised the consultant. "I think she's got pneumonia, and she's very dehydrated. Her pulse is" and gave him details, and Jerome nodded, as he examined her. "I'm sure you are right. She definitely needs antibiotics, and probably admission to hospital, to get some fluids into her. I'm going to phone one of my medical colleagues, and he can make a decision," and he went out into the sitting

room. Alexandra started coughing again, and while she was awake, Bea took the opportunity to get some fluids into her. She drank thirstily, then started coughing again, and Jerome came back into the bedroom. "My colleague wants her to be admitted, so I'm going to take her to hospital" he said. "Can you get her ready for the journey please?" and he watched as Bea started to find something to wrap her in. Her dressing gown was on the back of the door, and she walked over to get it, to see Jerome staring intently at the photo on the wall opposite the bed. He didn't say anything, just looked down at the woman lying on the bed, and fingering her hair. Bea wrapped Alexandra into her dressing gown, and Jerome scooped her into his arms. "She doesn't weigh anything" he muttered, and Bea nodded. "I've told her she's much too thin. She's lost a lot of weight since she left St. Anselm's." she agreed. "Is it okay if I come with you?" and he nodded.
"She'll need somebody to be with her, if you wouldn't mind staying."
"I don't mind staying with her, but I'm meant to be on duty at 1.00pm, but she'll probably be admitted to my ward anyway, so I should be able to be with her, and still go on duty."
The journey to the hospital was short, and Alexandra was soon being examined by one of the medical officers. As Bea had guessed she would be, she was admitted to Bea's ward, and was soon tucked up in bed, with a drip in place, giving her fluids, IV antibiotics working, and her hair tied back, making her look very young. Bea kept a very close eye on her all that evening, whilst undertaking her other

duties, and when Jerome visited her later that evening, she was able to tell him that Alexandra's temperature was slightly down, the cough had lessened and her breathing was easier. "Are you able to have a talk with me tonight, or would you rather leave it until tomorrow?" he asked, "I know you'll be busy tonight, but I would like to have a serious chat with you."

"If you can wait until the night staff, come on, I'll give them the report, and then we could have a talk then, if that would be okay." Bea answered, wondering what Jerome was going to ask, but she had a fairly good idea about that and knew it would ultimately be a good thing for her friend. "That's fine" he agreed. "I'll go and phone my wife, and tell her where I am, and then do some work in my office, and I will come back and talk to you when the night staff come on." They agreed, and he disappeared to go to his office. When the night staff came on duty, he returned, and went into the relatives' room to wait for Bea to come and talk to him. She entered the room, holding a couple of mugs of coffee, and handed him one, and gestured for him to sit. "Okay, what do you want to know?" she asked him, as she sank down into one of the armchairs.

"Firstly, what's her real name?" he asked and her eyebrows rose.

"What do you mean?"

"You called her Alex several times today, but I've always known her as Alison, so what is her proper name?" Bea sighed, but knew she had to tell him the truth, and hoped that Alex would forgive her.

"I've known her since we started training together,

and her full name is Alexandra Louise Taylor-Ellis. What name do you know her by?"
"Alison Turner" he said. "But, if her real name is Alexandra Taylor-Ellis, why did she change it?"
"She told me that when she left her husband, she didn't want him to be able to find her again, even if he wanted to, which she doubted, because she thought he was having an affair with somebody else, so she changed her name, altered her appearance, and moved away from him. She still loves him, but doesn't want to contact him, but I think you know some of this anyway, don't you?" he nodded and she went on, "You're not going to tell him that she's here are you?" he shook his head. "No, even though it might help him. It wouldn't be fair on her, would it? She looks dreadful at the moment, and I'd like her to be well, before they get back together. Anyway, he's abroad again at the moment."
"Does he still love her?" Bea asked and Jerome nodded. "She saw somebody she thought was him with another woman, and got the wrong impression. It wasn't Damien, it was Steven, who is our brother, kissing his wife Leila, but he's never been given the opportunity to be able to tell her."
"So, let me get this right," Bea said, "Alex is married to Damien, and Steven is married to Leila. Alex thought she saw Damien kissing Leila, but it wasn't him, it was Steven, and she got the wrong impression and left him. Since then, she's been on her own, thinking that her husband doesn't love her anymore, and she's eating her heart out, not being able to talk to Damien and get his side of the story" Jerome nodded, and Bea shook her head. "I can see

how she managed to get the wrong impression, and knowing Alex as I do, I can also see why she won't contact Damien to ask him to explain. I can't understand either, why he never told her that he was part of a set of identical triplets." Jerome laughed, and explained that his brother had wanted to surprise her, when they eventually met. "That backfired on him, though," he said, and Bea laughed and agreed, before continuing, "However, you don't know the other part of the story. She knows now that it was Steven and Leila, not Damien and Leila, she found that out, when she met up with Steven and saw him with Leila, but she doesn't want to go back to living with Damien, if he's going to continue as he did when they were married, because he was never there."

"He's promised to change if they ever get back together, and give up some of his overnight stays abroad, or take her with him."

"But even that's not going to help her much. She told me about her life when she was with him, and I wasn't at all impressed, I can tell you! She told me he was never at home, he spent more time abroad, than he did with her. Apparently, he was abroad or away for nearly six months of the eleven they were married! Believe me, I wouldn't have stood for that! She also told me all about some of the receptions she attended with him, which he insisted she go to. She was always the youngest person in the room. After they'd eaten, the men would go into another room to talk together, and if the other women deigned to speak to her, the only thing they talked about was the difficulty of getting good help in the home, or their grandchildren, but mostly they didn't talk to her anyway. They were often foreign as well, and half the time they would speak together in different languages, and she didn't understand them, so she would spend most of the evenings without anybody to talk to, and she'd be by herself all evening. Apparently, she went to one, where she said good evening to the hosts and that was that for the entire evening. They didn't even say goodbye to her! Nice manners, I don't think! But the biggest problem was when she was at home – the housekeeper tried to control her. She wouldn't let her do anything in the flat, no housework or cooking or anything like that, all her laundry was done for her, but she didn't like Alex being in the flat during the day, so she would have to go out, and I've now found out that the woman was also controlling who she saw or spoke to. I phoned her frequently, was told she was never in, when she was, I left messages that I was assured she was getting, and they never got passed on. She never got given the letters or the cards I sent to her either. I visited the flat and was assured that she was always out. I assumed she would have been abroad with Damien, but that turned out not to be so. That happened to other friends as well. Their messages were never passed on. No wonder she thought that everybody had deserted her. I couldn't understand why Damien had changed so drastically. I saw them together before they married, hell, I was a witness at their wedding, and he always seemed so attentive to her, he couldn't keep his hands off her, but he must have changed dramatically after they were married. She told me she was so bored and lonely most of the time, and after hearing everything, I can understand why! She had found somewhere to do voluntary work, wanted to be able to do something to pass the time, but when she told Damien what she was going to do, he didn't want her do anything, because he said she wouldn't be available if he wanted to take her away at very short notice, so she gave up the idea of working, but after all that, he never took her anywhere! There's a limit to how many times you can go shopping or how many books you can read. Is it any wonder she wants things to change, if she goes back to him? She's been so unhappy lately. She's lost so much weight, she looked ill before she got this infection, but now she looks even worse and I've never seen her so thin. She's dyed her hair and it looks horrible. She was blonde before, that's her natural colour, but I don't think anybody would give her a second look at the moment."

Jerome nodded. He had known some of the problems that Damien and Alexandra had been having, but didn't realise how bad her life had been, for Damien had never told him the full story. "I don't know why Damien changed so much either, but Bea, couldn't her parents have helped her?" he asked, but Bea shook her head. "She was orphaned when she was 14 or 15. Her parents were killed in a car crash, and she was the only child. After their death, she was sent to a children's home, and she didn't have many friends there. I don't think there was much money left either, so she's had to make her own way in the world, and support herself. She never told me much about her childhood, even though we got very friendly when we were training together."

"How do you think she would feel, if Pandora and I invited her to stay with us, when she's discharged?" he asked, but Bea shook her head. "She wouldn't accept, fearing that she would see Damien. I'll get one of the social workers to come and talk to her, and see if we can sort something out for her," but Jerome shook his head. "Tell the social workers, that I'll pay for her to go to a hotel, and be looked after, and hopefully she can get better, and put on some weight. Make up some story about hospital workers being cared for when they're not well, and when she comes back to work, I'll arrange a meeting for her with Damien, after I've got some assurance from him, that he makes it definite that he'll give up his travelling, or most of it. He can't go on like this, he's got to realise that his marriage should mean more to him, than his job. But I think he knows that anyway!" He smiled at Bea. "Thanks for your help today, Bea, and thank goodness you tried to phone her, and got worried when she didn't answer. She could have died without our intervention, and then she'd never have known how much Damien loves her, and he'd have been inconsolable, for she means so much to him. He's been searching for her since she went, and he's changed – not so light hearted if you know what I mean."

Bea stood up. "I'm glad you're going to help look after her. Let's hope she doesn't hate me when she's better, for having told you all her problems." she glanced at her watch. "I must go home," she said, "I'm on an early duty tomorrow morning, but I'll just go and see how Alex is, before I go."

"I'll come with you, then I'll drive you home"

"Thank you" she replied, and they went into the ward to see how Alexandra was faring. Her breathing was easier, and when Bea touched her forehead, she was relieved to see that her friend's temperature was lessening. "I'll see you tomorrow" she whispered to the night nurses, and they left the ward. Jerome drove her to her flat, before returning to his own house, and told Pandora all about Alexandra and how ill she had been, for he had given her the barest details when he phoned earlier. "I can't believe she's been working for you for the last few months, and you didn't know it was her," Pandora said, after she had listened to her husband's tale, but Jerome shook his head. "Remember, I've only ever seen her in a couple of photos, and not many of them either. Damien keeps them to himself, there are none on display, and I must admit I'd forgotten her face. She didn't seem at all familiar when she started working for me. Must be the hair. I didn't realise how hair colour can alter somebody's appearance so much." Pandora smiled at her husband's admission, and resolved never to dye her hair. "Mind you," he continued, "she's got a photo of the pair of them, on the wall of her bedroom in the flat, and she looks totally different, so happy and relaxed. She's got more flesh on her bones, and my brother looks so very much happier than he has done for a long time. It must have been taken on their honeymoon, when they went up to Scotland. They both look so much in love." he sighed, wondering how he was going to affect a reunion, then grinned. "I'd been to her flat when I was trying to locate Nanny Trotter, and she invited me in for coffee, told me a little bit about herself, that she'd been living with a man, but she didn't think that he wanted her anymore, and when I was leaving, I remember thinking what an idiot he must have been." He and Pandora laughed about that, then she asked "So how are you going to get them back together when she's better?" for she liked her brother-in-law and would like him to be happy with Alexandra if they could be reunited. "I have absolutely no idea" he answered. "But I'm hoping I can think of something before I have to do it. I'll have to talk to Damien before that, as well, and get his assurances that he's going to give up some of his travelling, or take her with him. I did wonder about getting her to come back here to convalesce, but her friend Bea thinks that she would refuse, in case she saw Damien. The least I can do is make sure she goes somewhere to convalesce where she'll be looked after. At least she's in the right place now. Let's hope she gets well soon." and he gave Pandora a hug. "And let's hope we can make Damien see the error of his ways" she answered. "Your brother is a bit of an idiot in some ways."

"I couldn't agree more." Jerome said, "Come on, let's have an earlyish night for once." and Pandora agreed.

Chapter Nine

Alexandra woke in the night, feeling a bit better than she had done the previous day. Her throat was less painful than it had been, and her cough hadn't kept her awake. She looked around her, and realised she was in hospital, for she could see other patients in the neighbouring beds. It was still dark, so knew it must still be very early. She couldn't remember coming to hospital and wondered how she had got there. She yawned, and closed her eyes again, and the next thing she knew, Bea was standing by her side, reading a thermometer, which had obviously registered her temperature, and feeling her pulse. "What's my temperature?" she whispered huskily, for her throat still hurt, "and why am I in hospital?"

"Don't you remember?" Bea asked, and she frowned and shook her head. "I had a cough, I remember that, and I didn't feel very well, so I went to bed. What am I doing here?"

"I phoned you yesterday morning, and knowing how you always answer your phone, when I didn't get a reply, I got worried, so I went to your flat. Your landlady took me up to your room, and I found you in bed, you looked absolutely awful, you were obviously very ill, and you've got pneumonia. Your boss got you admitted, and you've been here since yesterday afternoon. You're on antibiotics, you've still got a drip, so don't go moving that arm too much, but you've started to improve, and you're on the road to recovery." Alexandra stared at her friend, but Bea smiled at her. "Don't fret yourself" she said now. "You can have as much fluid as you like, so have a cup of tea, then go to sleep again. I'll still be here when you wake up again." and she helped her friend to sit up before handing her a cup of tea. "Drink that" she said. "Breakfast will be round in a few minutes, then you can have another sleep." Alexandra drank the tea her friend had given her, and waited for the breakfast trolley to come round, which it did shortly, and afterwards, she did as she had been told and went back to sleep. She appeared to still be asleep when Jerome came onto the ward to see her, and he smiled as he looked down at her. Bea came to join him at the bedside, and he acknowledged her presence. "She's looking a lot better today" he said softly, not wanting to disturb her sleep, and Bea nodded. "Her temperature is down, she's breathing better, and she hasn't coughed this morning very much, while she's been awake. I think we got to her just in time." she smiled, "I was extremely worried about her last night, and got in early this morning, just to see how she was. She'd be astonished if she knew that. I was never very good at getting up in the mornings, so to be in early, just to keep an eye on her, would be a great shock to her."

"You're right about that. Thanks Bea." Alexandra's voice was husky, but her eyes were still shut. "Mr. Ellis, I'm sorry I won't be in work today. I'll be back tomorrow."

"Don't be ridiculous" Jerome was scathing, "you'll still be in here tomorrow, and when you're better, you'll take some time off to get properly well."

"Will you apologise to your brother for me not being

able to do any more work for him for a couple of weeks please"
"Alison, will you please stop worrying about work. Just concentrate on getting well again. Now, go back to sleep, and I'll see you soon." He went away then, and Alexandra opened her eyes, as Bea told her to take some tablets. "Don't fret" Bea said quietly. "He looked after you last night, when he bought you in, and it's obvious that he likes you. Now, take your tablets, then go to sleep again, and I'll wake you up later to have some lunch," and Alexandra did as she was told.

Alexandra was in hospital for seven days before she was discharged, for she would be on her own, and Bea wanted her to be kept in for as long as she could. The social worker had visited her, telling her that as she was a member of the hospital staff, she was eligible to spend two weeks at a hotel the hospital owned, on the south coast, recuperating completely, and she would be sent straight there, when she left the ward. So, she had asked Bea to collect some clothes for her, and on discharge, she was taken by hospital car, to Brighton, to the hotel. It was a large place, slightly old fashioned, but the staff looked after her like a queen, and she had to admit she felt a lot better than she had done, before her illness. She still had an occasional cough, but a fatherly doctor had examined her on her arrival at the hotel, and told her that it would soon go, and she would be completely well again. She spent her days at the hotel, not doing very much, reading or doing some embroidery, or when she felt like having some exercise, walking along the sea front, or round the town, examining the shops, for Brighton had some splendid antique shops, and she loved looking at them, deciding what she would buy for herself if she ever had a place to put them. She had been surprised to find that Bea had included her album of photos of Damien when she had packed her case, and was grateful, for although she had the pictures on her phone, she liked having photos she could hold, and she would have loved to see him. She admitted to herself that she still wanted him, loved him, and would like to talk to him again, even though she knew that if she did see him again, he would probably tell her he wanted a divorce. Although she was unhappy with her personal life, she found that she was able to eat well again, for she didn't need to cook for herself, and slowly she was regaining weight, and looking a lot better than she had done.

She had banked Damien's cheque before her illness, but not spent any of it, and now decided to buy herself some new clothes. She liked to look good, even if there was nobody to see, so spent most of it on a couple of new outfits. One was a deep blue dress, with a full skirt, and a pleated bodice, and it looked very good on her. She hadn't been able to resist it, even though she didn't know when she would be able to wear it, and decided she would dress for dinner that night, just to be able to wear it. The other was a pink day dress, fairly straight, reaching down to just below her knees, but she conceded to herself as she looked in the mirror of the shop, it suited her very well, and she would be able to wear it into the office. She bought shoes to match, and then, the money she had decided to spend, exhausted, went back to the hotel, more tired than she wanted to feel, and knew that she still needed time to recover. When she was back in the hotel again, she looked closely at her hair, and decided it needed to be coloured again, but she didn't want to try to get it done while she was away, so decided to leave it until she was back at work and could make an appointment with the hairdresser.

During her second week of convalescence, she contacted her solicitors, asking them if they had heard from Damien, but the answer was a negative. "What exactly did you say in your letter?" she asked, when she finally managed to contact them, for they had been very difficult to get hold of, never returning her calls, and she listened in disbelief as they read it. "For heaven's sake" she said, annoyed beyond belief at their answer. "That's not what I wanted you to say" she argued. "I asked you to tell him that if he wanted a divorce, I wouldn't contest it, not tell him that I actually wanted one. I knew the solicitor I spoke to, wasn't making a proper note of my requests. Can you write to him again, giving him that information and tell him that you made an error. I'm away from home now, but when I get back, I shall be into see you, and I will want to see a copy of the letter you send. I'm not very happy with the way you've dealt with my problems, as you can imagine, and I think I might be making a complaint about you to the Law Society." She put the phone down on them, without waiting for a reply, wondering if they

had made a bad situation worse, and knew she would be home shortly, and could deal with them in person. On her last day at the hotel, she received a phone call from Jerome, asking her how she felt, and she was able to tell him, with complete honesty, that she felt so much better, she would be returning to work on Monday morning. "Well, Patricia and I have been talking to Personnel about that, and because you've been so unwell, we'd like you to make your return in easy stages, so next week, we want you to come in for three days, Monday, Wednesday and Friday, afternoons only. We can discuss how to increase your hours when you're back. So, I'll see you on Monday afternoon."
"But I'm better now" she insisted, but he was adamant.

When she returned to the hospital on Monday afternoon, and had done an afternoon's work, she was glad he had insisted on her doing reduced hours, for by the time she got home that evening, she was exhausted. There had been a lot of work waiting for her, and she looked at the desk with despair, wondering how she was ever going to be able to get it all done, for Jerome had been insistent that she take as much time to recover as she needed. The most important correspondence work had been done by somebody else, but there was still a lot to catch up with. She had been glad to be able to see Mrs. Megson again, when she got back from the hotel, although the old lady appeared to be slightly hesitant about talking to her, and she knew, without being told, that her landlady had decided to sell the house, and she would have to find new accommodation, for she knew she would be asked to move out. She decided there and then to try and find somewhere else as soon as she could.

She was not working on Tuesday, so went to the shop where she had originally found details of Mrs. Megson's flat, and visited the towns' estate agents, but there was nothing she liked, at a price she could afford, so went back into work on Wednesday lunchtime, wondering where she could find another place to live. The old lady had not said anything, but she wanted to be prepared if she were to be given notice to quit, and wondered if she might have to move to a different area, away from the hospital, and involving a bus ride into work each day, a prospect she wasn't looking forward to. She had also made an appointment with the solicitors for Thursday afternoon and was gearing herself up for a very forthright discussion with them.

Jerome was at home with Pandora on Tuesday evening, and had contacted Damien, earlier in the day, to find out whether, he would be available the following day and persuading him to come and have dinner with them. His brother had visited the couple, over the weekend, and had told them that he was now on a few weeks leave from the office, and showing them the letter he had received from Alexandra's solicitors. In it, the solicitor had apologised for the previous letter, when they had given him some erroneous information, and Damien told his brother that he felt slightly better about the situation, but wondered why they hadn't responded to the letter he had sent them, not knowing that a fire in the post box had been responsible for its non-arrival, and had decided he would visit them soon, to talk to them, and discuss the situation. To that end, he had made an appointment with them for Thursday afternoon and hoped they would be able to help him. He was sitting with Jerome and Pandora at their dinner table that evening, when he informed the couple, he had told his colleagues, that following his holiday, he was rearranging the way he worked, and would not be available to travel to foreign parts at moment's notice, and had told them that they would have to find somebody else, somebody preferably unmarried, to fulfil that obligation, and he had rearranged the way he would work in future. Jerome had stared at his brother. "You meant that?" he said, and Damien had nodded as he replied "Certainly I meant it. I told them months ago, but some of these trips were planned, so I had to honour them, and the others were urgent. I know that I ruined any chance of having a happy life with Alexandra because I wasn't at home, and what with my housekeeper treating her as she did in the flat, I can understand why she felt she had to go. To have seen somebody she thought was me, kissing another woman, must have been the final straw. I just wish I could tell her that it wasn't me, explain everything, and ask her if we could try again. Seeing you and Pandora and Steven and Leila together, has made me realise what I'd lost when she went. I knew I'd ruined everything before that anyway, but just seeing you pair, and your wives made it all so much more real. I

should have told her all about you and Steven, but I kept your existence a secret, because I wanted to surprise her, and I deserve everything that has happened since." he sighed deeply. "Do you think I'll ever be able to see her again?" he asked. "I've had no luck tracing her, and she seems to have disappeared off the face of the earth. The solicitors won't help, when I spoke to them, they just said they would deliver any letter I wanted to write to her, but I want to see her, to talk to her, and try and convince her, that it wasn't me she saw." Pandora patted his hand. "Don't worry Damien, I'm sure you'll meet again, don't you Jerome?"
"Oh, I definitely think you'll meet up again" said his brother complacently. "Now, come and have coffee before you go home" and the three of them had gone to sit by the fire and talk about other things.

That evening, when Damien had gone back to his flat, and they were alone, Pandora asked her husband what he was going to do, and Jerome grinned wickedly at his wife. "I'm going to get him to visit the hospital tomorrow. I'm going to phone him, telling him I've had some information about Alexandra's whereabouts, and when he gets there, I'm going to open her office door, usher him in, and wait for the shouting to stop." Pandora laughed at her husband's explanation. "As I'm not working tomorrow, I think I might just come and visit you, you can introduce me to Alexandra, I'll invite her to dinner with the entire family and then wait around to see what happens" she said cheerfully, and Jerome agreed to her visit.

On Wednesday afternoon, Alexandra went into the office again, looking at the pile of papers on her desk, before getting on with the work that awaited her. She was wearing the pink dress she had bought when she was away, and she had seen that Jerome's eyes had registered that she looked good. She had sorted everything to her satisfaction, and got through quite a bit of work, when the door opened, and she looked up to see Jerome, escorting a very good-looking woman. "At last, I can introduce you" he said, "Alison, this is Pandora, my wife." The two women shook hands, "Pleased to meet you at last, Alison," said the model. "We must all get together soon. The boys want to say a big thank you for getting them together again, but I know you've not been well, and we've had to put it off, but you're better now, so what about a day next week?" Although Alexandra did not want to accept an invitation, she knew she would have to, but she did not plan on going. Finally, she agreed a date with Pandora, said her farewells, and then got on with her work, as Jerome led his wife back to his own office. "Have you phoned him yet?" she asked but he shook his head. "I'm just going to do it now. Time him to see how long it takes him to get here" he grinned at her and picked up the phone. Damien was at home, and listened with astonishment, as his brother said he'd been given some information about Alexandra's whereabouts and to come immediately and was soon driving to the hospital. He went straight to Jerome's office and begged to know what information his brother had been given. "Well, I met somebody who used to work with her" Jerome said, his face unsmiling, but his eyes gleamed with amusement. "Come and have a talk to her", and he stood up, and led his brother to Alexandra's office. "She's in here" he said, opened the door, ushered his brother in, and shut the door behind him.

Alexandra looked up as the door opened, went very white, stood up, and stared in astonishment at the figure of her husband who stood in the doorway. He stared at her, hesitated, then smiled brilliantly at her. Neither of them said a word, she was unable to, for she was so shocked to see him, in this, her place of work, as Damien came swiftly towards her, took her in his arms, hugged her close to him, bent his head, and kissed her as he had never kissed her before. The kiss lasted a very long time, and although Alexandra knew she shouldn't be kissing him back, she did so for she felt at peace when she was in his arms. At length he raised his head and stared down into her eyes. "Oh my God" he breathed, "At last, I've found you. Oh Xandra, my darling girl, I've missed you so much. I love you so much, and I didn't know what to do when you disappeared. I wanted to talk to you, to tell you it wasn't me you saw, but I couldn't find you to tell you. You seemed to disappear into thin air. Oh, my darling, I'm so sorry for everything that happened. It was all my fault. I'd taken on too much work in the office, and that was why I was never at home, but I didn't realise you were being bullied by that old harridan who worked for me. I didn't know she was making your life such a misery. Can you find it in your

heart to forgive me?"
Alexandra pulled back from him, and reluctantly, he allowed her to move. "I don't know" she said now. "I know now, it wasn't you kissing Leila, it was Steven, but you never told me about your brothers, or the fact that you're identical, did you? And when we were together, you didn't seem to listen to anything I said. I told you I was fed up living in that flat when you weren't there, but you didn't change did you? Do you know, that in the eleven months we spent living together, you were away for nearly six of them?" her voice rose slightly and got louder. "You missed my birthday, wouldn't take me out when you got home, because you were tired after a long trip abroad, and I was so bored, because I had absolutely nothing to do. I couldn't do any housework, or laundry, that horrible woman did everything, and although you were very generous and gave me money to spend as I wanted, I was very lonely. You were never there, and when you were at home, we didn't do anything together. You were always working in your office, so we didn't even spend the evenings together. I couldn't do any voluntary work, because you didn't want me to be unavailable if you wanted to take me away, as I'd probably be working. But you didn't take me away either did you?" Her voice spiralled upwards, and she knew she was going to yell at him, if she continued. He bent his head and kissed her again, then said "go on" when he lifted his head again. She drew in a deep breath, felt her temper recede slightly and continued, "You wouldn't listen to me, when I told you how I felt, and then accused me of not wanting to go to any of those

horrible receptions with you. They were awful, nobody ever talked to me, and I couldn't wait for the evenings to come to an end. And now I've found out from Bea, that that despicable woman was taking phone messages and not passing them onto me, destroying letters that were sent to me, and telling my friends who visited the flat, that I wasn't in, so I thought they didn't want to continue their friendships with me. I was so lonely Damien. You were very distant with me, and I felt as if you'd fallen out of love with me, you weren't always there anyway, and she didn't want me in the flat. I felt like an intruder. I met her once again, after I left you, you know, and she smirked, and told me that she was glad I'd gone, because she didn't think I was right for you, and now she had you all to herself again! I always wanted to live in a house in the country, with dogs and cats, and children, and I had told you that, but you didn't seem to listen to me. Instead, we lived in that flat, which was downright luxurious, but I couldn't have any pets, and we'd decided we weren't going to have children just yet." she paused for breath, and Damien took her into his arms again, and kissed her silent, so that her resentment at his treatment vanished, and she kissed him back. When he lifted his head again, she pushed her head against his shoulder, as he cuddled her close to his body. "I'm so very sorry my darling" he said, and she relaxed against him. "I know the faults have been on my side, and I promise that if you come and live with me again, I'll change." He kissed her again, and she smiled. "When we're together like this, everything seems okay, but then you go back to working all the

hours God sends, or you go abroad, and everything's wrong again." He nodded. "I've already decided to change my way of working, and I'll be able to stay at home with you, and you'll never be lonely again." She smiled up at him. "I'm so glad about that, for I couldn't go on as we had been doing Damien. When I found out from Jerome, that you were looking for me, wanting to search the register to see where I was working, I thought that you wanted to divorce me, which is why I told my solicitors to write to you to tell you that I wouldn't object, but they sent you the wrong letter. When I finally managed to contact them when I got out of hospital, I told them to write to you again, and apologise, and tell you that they'd sent the wrong information. Did they do that?"
He nodded, then said worriedly "Why were you in hospital?"
"Remember, about three or four weeks ago, you went to Nanny Trotter's house where I was living, to thank me for doing your typing? I didn't feel very well that evening, as I'd got a sore throat, and a cough, and it was that weekend that I became very ill and got pneumonia. Bea came and found me and got Jerome to admit me to hospital and get me onto antibiotics."
"Oh, my darling, you poor thing. But you're better now?" he asked, kissing her again, and she nodded, before he said, "What do you mean, I came to thank you for doing the typing? Were you doing it?"
"Of course I was. Who do you think Jerome's secretary is?" he looked astonished at her revelation, and she continued. "That's why I phoned Jerome, after I'd seen Steven, because you would have

recognised my voice. I thought it was you I bumped into in the High Street, realised it couldn't have been, because you'd have recognised me, then the next day, I met the man, who I now know, to be Steven, again. I was having a coffee; he came over to ask if he'd hurt me after bumping into me the day before. He said he was waiting for his wife, and when she came in, I recognised her as the woman I'd seen you kissing, or thought I'd seen, when I saw them in town, the day after we had that big argument, and the day before I left the flat and you. He called her Leila, and it was after that, I realised it couldn't have been you after all, and knew I'd just spoilt any chance we had of getting back together, because that was the day after I'd asked the solicitors to write to you. They said they'd already sent you the letter." She took a deep breath. "I do love you Damien, I always have done, and when I thought you wanted to divorce me, I was very upset. Even Jerome noticed and wanted to know who or what had upset me." He hugged her close, kissed her then lifted his head and stared down at her face. "How long have you been working for Jerome?" he asked and when she replied "Since he started here. About four months now" he looked puzzled then said, "So why didn't he tell me you've been working for him for that time? He knew I've been looking for you ever since you left me. Hell, he even said he was helping me!"

"He didn't know it was me because I've been using a different name. I don't know how he found out that I was your wife."

"That's something I'm going to have to talk to my brother about" he said grimly, and kissed her again,

holding her body close to him. "I'm so very sorry my darling" he said again, "I never wanted to make you unhappy." he hesitated, "I had decided to change my way of working, and make sure I was able to be with you more often, but will that make any difference to how you feel?" She nodded, happy to be in his arms again, and knew he was trying to make her life more pleasant. "It's because you were never at home, that I got really upset, and what with the fact that I thought you'd found somebody else, well, that's the reason I had to go. I'm so glad you got rid of that horrible woman you had as a housekeeper" she said knowing he was going to question her knowledge.
"I got rid of her when I found out what she was really like. You'd been gone for a few months, I couldn't find any trace of you, I couldn't even speak to Jerome very often, because he was abroad, and one evening, I was feeling very depressed, and she tried to cheer me up but made some very disparaging comments about you. I lost my temper with her, and it was then she told me she didn't think that you were right for me, so she'd done her best to make you unwelcome, and confessed what she'd done to you. I lost my temper when I heard that, told her a few home truths, and dismissed her immediately. She seemed so good, when she first came to work for me. My new housekeeper is a lovely lady called Emma. She'd look after you very well, if I wasn't there, and allow you to do anything you wanted. But how did you know?" She smiled at him. "I know Emma. I met her when she fell over and injured her ankle, and I helped her and waited with her for the ambulance. We got friendly, and she gave me her

address, and asked if I could meet up with her again. When I got home, I looked at the address she had given me, and saw it was your flat, and I nearly fell over." she grinned as she reached up and kissed him, and he kissed her back, "It was you!" he exclaimed. "When she told me about the help she'd had, I wanted to meet you, to thank you for looking after her, but she didn't have your address." She nodded and grinned at him. "I wasn't going to give her the address, just in case she passed it on to you, and you went to the flat." He nodded, and kissed her again, before she continued, "I made a point of finding out from Jerome, when you were going to be away, before I could meet up with her again. It was Emma who told me you'd been very upset when you got a solicitor's letter telling you that your wife wanted a divorce, which is when I found out that they'd sent you the wrong letter. But did you really mean it, that you would change your way of working?"

"Xandra my darling, I told my colleagues months ago, that I was changing my way of working, and they were going to have to find somebody else to do the overseas trips, and preferably somebody who was unmarried, because that was what had caused my marriage to fail."

"So, you won't have to go abroad for long trips anymore?" she asked but he shook his head. "I might have to go abroad occasionally, but I'd make sure you came with me, and I'd arrange for us to go on sightseeing trips while we were away. You won't have to go to any more receptions either unless you want to. I obviously didn't listen properly, when you told me what they were like for you. I'm so sorry my darling. I've arranged everything so that I can work from home, and only go into the office occasionally, so I can be with you most of the time. I take it you still don't have a passport?"

"I do" she smiled at him, "I'd arranged to get one before I left you, and it arrived the day I left the flat and you, and I've not managed to use it yet. I did it as a surprise for you. And" she said, staring at his well-loved face, "talking of surprises, why on earth didn't you tell me you were one of three identical brothers? It would have made life a bit easier for me, if I'd known, and I'd have realised it wasn't you kissing another woman."

"I know that now. I was hoping to give you a very big surprise when you met up with Jerome eventually, because I wanted to see the shock in your face, when you met him, but that backfired on me. I'd arranged for you to meet my mother along with David, Elizabeth and Marie, but then I had to go abroad, so we didn't manage to meet up with them. Jerome was out of the country at the time, and of course we had no idea where Steven was, so I never told you, and odd as it sounds, I didn't have any photos of the three of us together." he hugged her close, "Oh Xandra my darling girl, can you ever forgive me? I've never stopped loving you. I'm so very sorry I treated you as I did. I didn't realise until it was too late, how bad life must have been for you. If you can come and live with me again, I'll take you with me wherever I have to go, and we'll be able to have a home in the country with children and dogs and cats, and I'll do everything I can, to make you happy for the rest of your life. I love you so very

much my darling" and he bent his head to kiss her again, as he held her close against him.
"Yes" Alexandra said when he finally lifted his head, and she got her breath back. "Yes, I can forgive you, but if you ever hurt me like that again, I'll go so far away, that nobody will ever find me."
"I won't give you the opportunity" he said, holding her close to him and kissing her. She had her arms around his neck, his lips were on hers, and she didn't hear the door behind her open, for she was wrapped in his arms, but Damien did, and he lifted his head, said "Thank you" to his brother, and went back to kissing her again, until she suddenly registered the fact that Jerome and Pandora were standing in the doorway, watching, and tried to pull away. Damien wouldn't let her go, and Jerome smiled as he saw how embarrassed she appeared to be. "Oh hell," Jerome said suddenly, "this means I'm going to have to get another secretary. I almost wish I hadn't bothered" and they all laughed. "You've been a good secretary Mrs. Taylor-Ellis, but you'll be an even better wife to Damien." he said and smiled at her. Damien hugged her close, and she smiled at Jerome and Pandora, looking extremely happy to be in his arms. "You're going to have to get your hair back to its natural colour. It really doesn't suit you, being that colour." Damien said, as he ran his fingers through her hair, and pulled the pins out, so that it fell neatly on to her shoulders, and she nodded. "I didn't know how else to disguise myself when I left you. The dye has started to wear out anyway, and it would have needed to be done again" she said. "But I couldn't do it sooner, because I wasn't very well,

and apparently when you've been ill, the dye doesn't take, and the colour goes quicker. Hopefully, I'll be able to go to a hairdresser and get it back to normal soon." She turned to her brother-in-law. "So, who told you?" she asked. "Somebody had to have done, because I know I didn't say anything." Jerome smiled at her as he drew Pandora closer to him, "When you were so ill, Bea was looking after you, calling you Alex, instead of Alison, which is the name I knew you as, so the evening you were admitted, I asked her to explain, and the first thing I wanted to know, was your correct name. She told me then that you were Alexandra, but of course, I'd seen the photo of the pair of you, in your bedroom. But there were times before that, when I became suspicious - you had said you had lived in a large flat in Richmond and you hadn't worked, and then when you were talking on the phone when you put us on to Steven's whereabouts, I asked you what you would have done, if you wanted to hide, and you said you'd have changed your name, altered your appearance, and moved away. Then you phoned me instead of Damien, after we'd been to your flat, despite him having left his number. And of course, you're a trained nurse as well, which didn't make sense to me, that you'd stopped nursing. Also, Nanny Trotter said a few things, things that she couldn't have known unless you'd told her, and I became very suspicious. But I think the final piece of the puzzle came after you'd opened the envelope from Damien, after you'd done his typing, containing the cheque, and a note from him. You were looking so upset afterwards, where you'd been happier beforehand, and things

started to click into place. I was going to ask you outright, when you came back from your leave, but I was busy, and then you became ill, and I couldn't."
Damien hugged her to him again, "Did my note upset you?" he asked, and she nodded. "It was the sight of your handwriting that made me upset. It bought back some very happy memories and made me cry."
He bent his head to kiss her again. "When can you leave here?" he asked her as he lifted his head again. "We've got a lot of catching up to do, and I don't want to have to share my wife with my brother, sister-in-law, and a load of typing!"
"I'm meant to work until 5.00 pm, but I'll ask Patricia, if I can go earlier" Alexandra said, and was interrupted by Jerome. "Don't bother asking, I'll tell her everything, and that I've sent you home with your husband. She'll understand, because she wanted you to be happy." Alexandra left Damien's arms, and went to her brother-in-law, and kissed him on the cheek. "Thank you" she said simply and went back to Damien. "Get your coat" he said, "We're going home. I'll phone you sometime" he informed his brother, and Jerome and Pandora were smiling as they watched as Alexandra donned her coat, grabbed her handbag, and he guided her out of the room.

Seventeen months later, Alexandra and Damien walked hand in hand along a deserted sandy beach on the Island of South Uist in the Outer Hebrides. They were happy, tanned and relaxed, for the summer had been an exceptional one, with days of endless sunshine. "You know most of our friends think we're crazy to have bought a holiday home up here on the edge of nowhere" he said, and she nodded. "It doesn't stop them trying to borrow it when they see how beautiful it is though, does it?" She grinned, "It'll be lovely to see Bea again tomorrow, when the plane gets in."

"Very thoughtful, our Bea" said Damien, "letting us have a couple more days to ourselves, before she and her husband visit, and we all have to go back to London next week. I hope they are going to be very happy. Still, by the time we get back, our new house will be finished, and we'll be able to move in. And everything will be ready when the baby arrives" He bent and kissed her gently. "I can't believe we almost lost this, through my stupidity in not telling you about the rest of the family. It'll be nice to see them as well, while we're still just a couple, for when the baby arrives, it'll be busy, and we won't have much time for entertaining." He put his hand gently on the small bump on her abdomen where their baby was growing and smiled at her. "We'll finally be a complete family with a baby, the first of as many as we want." He kissed her gently, then very hard, "Oh my darling Xandra, I love you so very much. Thank you for making me so happy." She kissed him back, and they stood together, with their arms around each other, looking out to sea. "I love you too Damien. I'm sorry that everything happened as it did, but I'm so glad Jerome intervened, and helped us to get back together. I'm so happy with you." she smiled, "Poor Jerome - when Pandora first told him she was pregnant, he was praying it wasn't twins, but their David is a lovely baby. And at last, Nanny

Trotter has forgiven him for stealing her thunder. She had it all arranged to get us back together, and he beat her to it! And now Leila and Steven's baby is due any day, much to her mother's delight. The whole family is expanding rapidly. I'm just so glad I'm not expecting triplets; twins will be bad enough" and she took a good look at his face and smiled as he assimilated what she had just said. "The midwife phoned me this morning with the scan results, while you were at the shop. I'll start having our family two at a time." He didn't say anything, just grinned widely, then kissed her hard, then took her hand and gently led her along the sand to their house on the edge of the beach.

THE END.

Printed in Great Britain
by Amazon

61111425R00102